W9-AGM-345

𝒜MERICAN 𝒮HORT 𝒻ICTION

Volume 1, Number 4, Winter 1991

LAURA FURMAN
Editor

BETSY HEBERT
SUSAN WILLIAMSON
Editorial Assistants

JOHN KINGS
Managing Editor

Editorial Advisory Board

ARTURO ARIAS	CYNTHIA MACDONALD
DAVID BRADLEY	JAMES MAGNUSON
ALAN CHEUSE	JAMES A. MICHENER
FRANK CONROY	ELENA PONIATOWSKA
ELIZABETH WARNOCK FERNEA	JUDITH ROSSNER
TONY HILLERMAN	LESLIE MARMON SILKO
FRANCES KIERNAN	TED SOLOTAROFF
JOSEPH E. KRUPPA	WILLIAM WEAVER
OWEN LASTER	WENDY WEIL

UNIVERSITY OF TEXAS PRESS

AMERICAN SHORT FICTION, established in 1991, is published four times a year by the University of Texas Press in cooperation with the Texas Center for Writers and "The Sound of Writing," a short story magazine of the air broadcast on National Public Radio. The editor invites submissions of fiction of all lengths from short shorts to novellas. All stories will be selected for publication based on their originality and craftsmanship.

STYLE *The Chicago Manual of Style* is used in matters of form. Manuscripts must be double-spaced throughout.

MANUSCRIPTS AND EDITORIAL CORRESPONDENCE Please send all submissions to: American Short Fiction, Parlin 14, Department of English, University of Texas at Austin, Austin, Texas 78712-1164. Manuscripts are accepted only from September 1 through May 31 of each academic year. Please accompany submissions with a stamped, self-addressed envelope.

SUBSCRIPTIONS (ISSN 1051-4813) Individuals/$24.00; Institutions/$36.00. Foreign subscribers please add $5.50 to each subscription order. Single Copies: Individuals/$7.95; Institutions/$9.00. Send subscriptions to: American Short Fiction, Journals Division, University of Texas Press, Box 7819, Austin, Texas 78713.

"The Golden Darters" by Elizabeth Winthrop and "Remembering Orchards" by Barry Lopez are published courtesy of "The Sound of Writing," a short story magazine of the air broadcast on National Public Radio.

Excerpt from poem "Apology for Bad Dreams" in "Remembering Orchards" by Barry Lopez: Copyright 1925 and renewed 1953 by Robinson Jeffers. Reprinted from *Selected Poems* by Robinson Jeffers, by permission of Random House, Inc.

Design, typography, and cover photograph by George Lenox

American Short Fiction

PUBLISHED IN COOPERATION WITH
THE TEXAS CENTER FOR WRITERS
Rolando Hinojosa Smith, Director,

AND WITH THE SOUND OF WRITING,
A SHORT STORY MAGAZINE OF THE AIR,
BROADCAST ON NATIONAL PUBLIC RADIO,
Caroline Marshall, Executive Producer

CONTENTS

THE EDITOR'S NOTES

With Issue 4, we come to the end of *American Short Fiction*'s first year of publication. It is easy to remember the moment in June 1990 when Susan Williamson and I sat in my academic office and tried to figure out how to start a quarterly. We read a box of manuscripts from "The Sound of Writing." We wrote fan letters to writers whose work we loved, editors whose achievements we knew, and agents we hoped to interest in *American Short Fiction*. The University of Texas Press sent an announcement to several writers' organizations, and within weeks we were receiving sixty or so manuscripts a day. Starting was no longer a problem. We were in the middle of an avalanche. In September, Betsy Hebert joined us, and Issue 1 was ready to go. I want to express my gratitude to Betsy and Susan for their hard work, politeness, and intelligence.

———

Some of the present issue comes from our first moments as a quarterly. The story by Elizabeth Winthrop, "The Golden Darters," and Barry Lopez's "Remembering Orchards" came to us through "The Sound of Writing." I liked Barry Lopez's story the first time I read it, but I can vouch for it as a story with legs. I've read it many times over the past months and have each time found something new in it. Annette Sanford and C. W. Smith are fellow Texas writers whose work I've read for years. Annette Sanford's "Helens and Roses" is my favorite of all her work; it is the story of a realistic marriage that never stops being romantic. C. W. Smith's "Witnesses" is a wonderful example of compression, and of form fitting content, for it is about the brief and tragic encounter of strangers.

John Rolfe Gardiner is a writer whose work I knew from reading *The New Yorker,* and I was pleased when his agent sent us his Portuguese story. I had the pleasure as an editor of stepping back and watching him take "The Magellan House" through different incarnations, until it reached its present form. He made radical changes and small ones, and all with the surest sense of what the story could lose and what it needed to keep.

Debra Jo Immergut and Tom Piazza both sent in their work early on, and we were attracted to their fresh voices, open but savvy characters, and humor in situations where other writers might find little. I am proud to be among the first publishers of their work.

———

Finishing *American Short Fiction*'s first year, I think of our writers, the editors who have recommended writers to us, and the agents who have sent us their clients' work. The world of letters is filled with competitiveness and in-soluble difficulties—there are more writers than top-notch places to publish, and some work is better than other work—but it is also a world of generosity, in which new work is welcomed and old friends are remembered. In the end, we are all readers, hoping for a good story.

THE SKIRT

After this summer with Liss, I feel a certain surrender. I am open to the next part of my life. And so through these white hot mornings I go, across the Mall behind government lawn-mowing squads, past late-season tourists browsing the snack carts for breakfast. I mount the marble steps to the great corniced box where I earn my pay. The security guard, who is dark-browed and angry, watches me. I pause outside the glittering glass doors and lift my face to the heavens, in contemplation.

Are you an American taxpayer? I spend your money. I am an assistant grants assessor in the Department of Education.

My name is Megan Rostow.

———

The summer truly began on June 19, the day of my murder fantasy. The air was wet and heavy in our lungs, brown blooms still clung to the azalea shrubs, and hazy light hung from a thick roof of clouds. We drove, Barry and Liss and I, out through the suburbs to the place where the Potomac drops from the Appalachian plateau to begin its mellow roll across the coastal plain. From parks along the banks, from rocky outcrops shaded by trees or jutting

over the water, you can watch the river's great tumble.
Seven frolickers drown there each year. When we clambered up to the rock's high shoulder, Liss gasped at the
view, and sidled to the very edge of the granite. She gazed
at the white thunder of the rapids below us. I, however,
stared at the shorts she wore. Cuffed above the knee, cotton, they were a butter yellow, printed with curly Venetian
gondolas. They were my mother's; she'd favored clothes
that told a story, sweaters with city maps woven into
them, dresses and slacks showing the signs of the zodiac
or the makings of a garden salad.

Mom had been bottom-heavy, and I noticed now that
Liss, in her twentieth year, was beginning to take after her.
She stood looking across the river, toward a sky the color
of somebody's shaven underarm. Her wiry red curls bent
in the wet wind. "Those shorts are not flattering," I called
to her over the water's tumult. She didn't hear me. But
Barry, propped next to me against a stove-warm boulder,
muttered, "Nice," as he opened a ragged paperback on
French legal history. He'd nestled a six-pack of beer alongside himself, his legs outstretched and ankles crossed, freed
from their tennis shoes. He was the picture of a pleasant
suburban outing. Liss sat down and dangled her legs over
the edge of the precipice, above the racing river. I rested
my head against the jagged wall at my back and shut my
eyes, and I pictured her disappearing beneath the snowy
water. Without blood, without screams, she'd slip under
the rapids and be gone.

The midday brightness soaked through my lids, and I
felt a leadenness that made my calves and forearms ache.
In the months following my mother's death this great
heaviness descended upon me for hours and days at a time.
Since Liss's arrival the previous week, I'd felt engulfed.
The river breeze riffling the fine hairs on the back of my neck
seemed to mock my inert heart. I opened my eyes and
rolled my head once more toward Liss. Her stretched-out

tank top had come untucked in back, her shoulders were round and pinkening, her elbows rough. I imagined it again, nudging her over the edge. She'd vanish in a twinkling. Barry would run over—I'd push him, too, take the car, head for somewhere far and anonymous.

I shut my eyes again and felt a queasy chill pass through me. I put my hand on Barry's warm leg. The wind tangled in the lush trees beyond our backs. And the afternoon passed uneventfully, heavy with water roar and lukewarm beer. When we returned home Liss discovered she'd been hired by Camp Victory for Teens at Risk.

––––

We are the living remnants of the Rostows and the Hallorans, Melissa and I. There are cemeteries in the downy suburbs of Columbus where weather-resistant flowers deck the rest of them. Our surname is also everlasting back home, bolted in red steel script above an office-supply store, the still-thriving business my grandfather began and my dad took over until his death by drowning in Jamaica, 1974. My mother sold the store to the floor manager, Mr. Otis.

A tricky, lovely, wonderful woman, my mother was. And quick, bright—she should have been on television. She opened her own tax preparation office instead. She never remarried, and it wasn't out of loyalty to my father; she searched, roaming the years with an open mind, but she never found anyone. The pain she must have felt, in that scrolled bed, night after night—for sixteen years! This thought knocks the wind from me. My mother's mother, Grandma Halloran, taught remedial reading right up until her death last year. Eight months after Grandma, last September, my mom was buried across town in the Rostow plot. The Rostows were a sprawling and attractive clan, but they lived in and around Leipzig, Germany, with a surplus of trust in the kindness of fate, or a puzzling lack of foresight. The exception was my grandfather David, who bolted across the Atlantic in '38 with his fat wife and small boy; the wife, Bella, and twin girls died in a lying-in hospital days after the U.S. entered the war.

Men of religion say death is a part of life, it's in the hands of God. I suppose I agree. But in the case of my mother, it seemed plain to me: the blame fell here, on earth.

———

When Liss found the summer job at Camp Victory, I was relieved. Not that I'd had time to worry about her; on my desk, piles of proposals trembled and shifted like the layers of the earth, people wanting grants to track the learning curves of Cambodians or home-schoolers or children who'd been driven by hunger to eat dirt and paint. I couldn't fret about my sister and whether she had the presence of mind to change trains at the right stop, to steer clear of the shooting neighborhoods, to lock the street door behind her when she got to my place. I simply wanted her to be busy and out of my way until she returned to college in Columbus.

In retrospect, I'm sure it was illegal for the camp to give her a bus route. When she drove home after her first day with the battered yellow van, I peered out the window at it. She dashed into the house, yelling, "You won't believe this."

"You can't drive kids around without a license," I said.

"The camp people tested me." She gathered her thick mop of hair in one hand and raised it off her neck, fanning herself with the other. "They think I can handle it." Her arms were rosy with sun. Down her loose sleeve I glimpsed a flesh-colored bra. Picking up an African violet from the windowsill, I pinched off some dead leaves. "You're hardly what I'd call responsible." I looked up at her, my chest tightening around my lungs. "Do these people know the first thing about you?" A flush rose in her face, her small bulbous nose. Her arms dropped to her sides and she stared at me a moment, eyes dark, lips slightly parted. I noticed she wore a thin gold chain of Grandma Halloran's. "You should probably mind your own business," she said, and she reached for a light blue towel that was hanging from a corner of a bookcase. She'd brought her own linens from school. "I don't believe anybody requested your opinion." She turned and walked down the hall, then I heard the bathroom door shut and the old plumbing groan and knock as the shower sputtered to life. Cupping velvety rotted leaves in one hand, I paused by the closed door on my way to the kitchen garbage can. Her sobs rung hollowly against the shower's tiled walls.

The galaxy of siblings is ruled by evershifting forces, balances changing and orbs drifting in and out of each other's sphere of influence. For years, Liss was living out her dramas across vast reaches of space from me. She met with expensive tutors; she wailed in her sleep and sleepwalked into walls; she got caught at every forbidden thing she did. The week she shoved a girl down a flight of stairs and was suspended from the seventh grade, I won a scholarship to a women's college in Virginia. She had never been my problem, I'd kept a clean distance from her messes, and once I left for school, she seldom occupied my thoughts.

But my mother's passing threw our planets out of whack. Early last December I received a letter from her, from the freshman dorm:

My roommate asked if I wanted to come home to Barberton with her for Christmas break. Her dad was just fired so it might be strange. Also, she said we'd have to go to church.

My mother had converted before her marriage, but her faith waned after my father's death and the holidays in our house passed aimlessly, without denomination. Liss, nine or ten years old, would beg to sleep over at a friend's house on Christmas Eve. Mom firmly refused: "They want to be with their own, and so should you."

Liss called me at work one morning soon after her letter arrived. "Your roommate sounds like fun," I said, my throat dry suddenly.

"Really?" Her voice was brittle and so clear she could've been standing right there in my cubicle. "You really think so?"

"I made plans to go to a friend's ski condo," I said. "There could be room for you, but I don't know . . ." When I hung up, my cheeks were hot with shame.

A week or so later the mail brought a ceramic incense burner with a postcard of a snowy Ohio scene tucked inside. "Happy Hanukkah/Christmas," it read. "Liss." I'll confess the use I found for the little perforated pot: holding Brillo pads beneath the kitchen sink. In return I sent a flowered scarf to Liss's dorm address, which was all I had. She wouldn't receive it until after New Year's.

———

When Liss's summer break rolled around, I didn't want to take her in. Barry said, "Megan, tell me something— where else can she go?" He and I met last Thanksgiving, at the feast of a colleague's family; he was the other stray. Though there was a difference between his orphanhood and mine: Barry's people (parents, aunts, step-uncles, cousins) were simply far away, in Pacific Palisades. Right off the bat, I knew his shining qualities—kindness, patience— were things I could use in my life. Even so I suspected, in the guilty private depths of my grief, that he'd one day become a relic of my recovery; like a swimmer clinging to the lip of the pool, once I regained my strength, I'd push off from him.

"My heart goes out to her," he said to me one night in

bed soon after Liss arrived. "She seems extremely forlorn." Then he kissed my stomach. In lovemaking, as in life, he was awkward, I thought—but his energy and earnestness impressed me. One evening in late June Liss brought home a snapshot, and sitting next to her on the couch, he pored over it with interest. Besides chauffeuring the Northwest D.C. van pool, she was assistant counselor to a group of twelve-year-olds, who'd posed for the group portrait standing on their heads. "What's this kid's name?" he said, pointing and scrutinizing. "She looks like she's thirty-five." His collar was unbuttoned, tie undone; his glasses rode low on his thin nose. Leaning in the doorway, I tossed a stack of mail onto the coffee table.

"She's an incest victim, foster child. She can't read at all." Liss looked up at me as I turned to leave the room. "Remember that stuttering girl Dana in my sixth-grade class?" she called after me.

"No," I said. In the bedroom now, I stripped off my skirt and my panty hose.

"This is the head counselor," I heard her say to Barry.

"Standing on his feet," he said. I pulled on cotton shorts, cherry red, and a T-shirt. I walked back into the room and he said, "New shorts." Liss set the picture facedown in her lap. "You've got great legs," she said. I bent to shuffle through the mail. "Mine are so sausagelike." She lifted a rather stubbly leg and extended it toward the coffee table, near my face.

"No, no, no," Barry said, with his unerring sense of what's required of him.

"Really?" Her voice brightened. "You think they're OK."

"Sure, they're very sexy," said Barry.

"I don't know. My shins don't taper," said Liss, stretching the limb up into the air now, narrowly missing my nose. "I'd say they're very shapely," protested Barry.

This conversation was making me nauseous, in the way

an extremely bad TV show sometimes will. I had to straighten up and leave the room, go to the kitchen, retrieve a crusted sticky bottle of tomato juice from the refrigerator, and pour myself a little, in order not to say something mean.

———

Some days later, on a dismal afternoon early in July, thunderclouds trolled the Mall with gray nets of rain. I emerged from work into the late afternoon, cringing beneath a ripped umbrella, and spied the van parked on the curb across the street, glowing brightly in the gloom like a gigantic canary melon. Liss cranked the window down and called to me. "We were passing by. I can give you a ride."

"I was going to stop at—" I gestured vaguely toward the shops down the block, but my feet in their low pumps were already soaked; around my ankles, my panty hose felt gummy. I splashed across the street and clambered into the passenger side, onto a moist vinyl seat. Liss had the driver's seat jacked up close to the wheel. A lone camper sat in the first long bench behind us. Liss turned to him as she waited for a break in traffic. "Robert, this is my sister Megan."

"Hey," he said, revealing braces. He was possibly fourteen years old, damp brown hair with long curls at the back of the neck, arrestingly large green eyes. On his T-shirt, the name LOPER was written in thick marker. He turned to stare out the window.

"Last on my route. He lives right over on Stanton Park." Liss struggled with the steering wheel, guiding the van's blunt nose through the rain-shimmering traffic. I couldn't recall being her passenger ever before. I turned back toward the boy. "Do your parents work on the Hill?" I regretted this reference to his family instantly—beatings, locked closets flashed luridly in my mind. But he answered evenly. "My dad's a Senate aide. My mother lives in Texas." He turned his face up as we passed the Washington Monument, its top hidden in clouds.

"My group won the pizza this week," Liss said, wiping condensation from the windshield.

"They cheated," said Robert. "I bet you anything." At a small apartment block facing the weedy park, Liss pulled up to the curb. She shifted in her seat to watch Robert swing open the door. "See you tomorrow?"

"Yeah," he said, stepping down to the wet street. He was taller than I expected, crouching and waving shyly through the doorhatch. "See you." He slammed the door shut. We watched as he dashed toward his building's broad awning, slinging a turquoise knapsack over his shoulder. His knees, poking out from khaki shorts, were knobby and tan.

"He seems normal enough," I said.

"Well," Liss frowned, shifting gears, negotiating a tortured U-turn on the narrow street. "He tried to kill himself in April." Before us, green branches arched soaked and glittering above the street. Through the watery windshield, everything seemed coated with gel. She reached to fiddle with the vents. A blast of air lifted her bangs, exposing her milky forehead.

"Why?" I said. "Anyone know?"

She shrugged. "Why not?"

I snorted at this. "Oh, grow up," I said. "You must be a wonderful influence." But as the words left my mouth I was visited by a sudden flood of sorrow, over the gulf between us, over her wan desperation. I fidgeted with the briefcase in my lap uncomfortably. She maneuvered into a parking space down the block from my apartment. Her mouth was working and her eyes bright as she turned off the ignition. All around us and above us leaves bobbed and winked in the rain. "I can't get what your problem is," she whispered.

"Basically," I said, hugging the briefcase to my chest, "I can't stand being around you." She nodded tightly at that, then yanked at the door handle, and almost fell out of the van. Pushing the door shut behind her, she walked up the glistening street toward my apartment, bowing her head to the rain.

When I was Liss's age, I had a bad freshman year at college. I felt poorly prepared by our public high school, badly dressed. Mom would call me every day. "It'll take some time. You'll start to love it," she'd say. "I'm so proud of you." I'd pictured her, coppery hair falling over the receiver in permanent waves, leaning against the kitchen counter, her lavender and black phases-of-the-moon pants smooth across her broad hips, her espadrilles, her gray eyes. I remember missing her terribly at those moments; I'd want to clutch her arms. Back then, I couldn't imagine my world without her.

During her freshman year, Liss took up poetry. She'd sent me a poem that arrived the day after Valentine's. I'd read the first lines,

> I cross shining ice-filmed snow,
> the soundless howl of solitude—

and dropped the sheet of paper with a shudder: "Oh God." Barry picked it up. "What's wrong?" He'd just arrived with white roses; red ones had come the day before. "I think she needs a boyfriend," I said, and ripped the tissue paper from the ivory blooms, arranging them in a vase with the others. They looked waxen, I thought as I stared at them. I knew that a bigger person than I would have forgiven her more readily. A better sister would have soothed her, shielded her from guilt. But when I'd arrived in Columbus last September, glimpsed Liss unkempt and alone in the airport, a wordless, airless fury tented around me, expanding as the reality of my mother's death—

and the stupid truths surrounding it—became plainer and plainer to me. I could muster no sisterly compassion: none when I listened to her recite a half-wrong prayer at the interment, and none when I left her five days later, on the opening morning of fall semester, among the other newly arrived freshmen on the front walk of a monolithic dormitory. She looked pale and tragic, waving good-bye with her clothes in bulging trash bags by her side. But what I felt as I watched her was, I'm sorry to say, something close to disgust. Because here is how it happened: Liss missed her be-home-by-two-o'clock curfew; my mother brushed against a gas burner while clearing away the dinner mess, then lay down in the adjoining den with a book. She could have made it until the curfew easily, they say. They think she could have made it until half past. But at three Liss was still searching for her lost car keys, after smoking joints with a locker-room attendant at the city pool, and it was 3:20 before she found them again. By then my mother, my rock and redeemer, was gone.

Gathering my umbrella and briefcase, I stepped out of the van and dodged black puddles up the front walk. Mom, Mom, she could almost be here. The circumstances that stole her from my life were, as you can see, so thin, so empty of significance—it made her achingly close to being alive.

———

The middle of July drifted past: dense sunshine dispersed by downpours, ragged men sprawled under the magnolia trees beside the Library of Congress. In the evenings and mornings the air was full of a limpid light that dulled the colors of the flowers and brought me close to tears as I walked back and forth from the Metro station with my suit jacket hanging over my arm. All the emotion of Liss's stay was beginning to wear me down. On July 23 I hit the office softball pool and won a weekend for two at Rehoboth Beach. Barry and I argued when I told him I was going alone. "I would like to know," he pleaded, his voice low in a restaurant, "why we are always proceeding on your terms—your terms." He leaned forward clutching the sides of his plate as if it were nailed to the table. I gazed at my meat, miserable. "As if I should proceed on anyone else's," I said. "I can't see why I should."

The weather at the seashore was flawless, and from my room on the high floor of a beachfront hotel the crowds in their bright scraps looked like flowering groundcover. Down on the boardwalk the smell of frying fat mixed with the briny air, the cries of birds and children, music from radios, and the electronic burping and honking of huge video arcades, backed by the rumble of the waves. I bought a lemon ice, spread my towel in the shade from the boardwalk, and sat with a book closed in my lap, watching the brown-shouldered lifeguards signal each other with flags, flinging a coded message from lofty chair to lofty chair, above the heads of the crowd. Soothed by the hiss and sizzle of retreating waves sliding back into the sea, I watched the doings around me and felt, finally, calm—more calm than I'd been in months, in the near-year since Mom died. I scraped the last of the ice from its waxy cup with the little wooden paddle and wondered if I should perhaps slow things down with Barry, if we should see less of each other. It was only fair. The idea descended over me like silk; I knew I was right. A sad lightness made my heart float.

A giggling toddler, pursued by a pretty woman in a modest, outmoded bikini, stumbled across a corner of my towel and tripped on my feet. Immediately he erupted in screams. The woman ran up and dropped to her knees, panting lightly, and scooped him up into her arms, cooing at him. "Lukie, Lukie, don't cry," she said, brushing sand first from his blubbery legs and then from my towel. She smiled up at me apologetically, laugh lines around her blue eyes. "He must be a handful," I said.

"Oh no, he's an angel." She stood up and cradled his head against her shoulder. "Aren't you, sweetie?" He'd stopped crying; pressing his cheek to her tan body, he looked at me with round eyes. "I'll get you a bomb pop," the woman crooned, carrying him off past blankets and blow-up water floats and striped umbrellas.

I thought of Liss, alone in my place back in the city. She most likely did not remember our two family visits to the shore in Maine. She would have been no older than that little boy. I vaguely recalled her spitting up as we ate sandwiches in a touring launch. She might assume she'd never seen the ocean. My mother and I had both avoided reminiscing about such times with my father; I suppose we feared it'd be too painful. But now, burying my wooden spoon in the sand, I suspected we'd simply hoarded those memories, my mom and I, guarding them jealously like tattered notes to be read in secret. When Liss used to knock on my bedroom door and ask me, Was his hair red-brown like hers or red-orange? Did he read all those books in the basement? I'd say, Why're you asking me, I can't remember. And Mom would give only the vaguest answers and say, He loved you very much, Liss, and you will always know that. At some point in her pubescence Liss quit asking about him, but by her bed she kept a dim gray baby portrait made in Germany.

I ended the weekend refreshed and relaxed, and not even the traffic crawling through fumes all the way from Kent Narrows to the far side of the Bay Bridge deflated my mood. Cutting across the city through the Sunday evening streets, I noticed how, even in the most destitute neighborhood near the football stadium, families smiled down at smoking barbecue grills, teen couples walked hand in hand, dogs romped, and trees shaded the streets with a dusky summer beauty.

As I turned the key in my front-door deadbolt I uttered a silent oath, that I'd try to inject a new tone into my dealings with my sister. I flung the door open and dropped my bag in the entry. "Liss? Hi!"

My bedroom door stood open down the dark hallway. I heard a hinge whine, and watched the door slowly close, as if under its own power. "Hi," Liss said from behind it. "I'm—I'll be right out, one sec." There was a strange quaver to her voice—she could have been jogging in place, or hopping.

"What're you doing in there?" My old swim-team windbreaker lay on the floor; I picked it up and hung it in the closet.

"I'm changing." I heard her moving behind the door as I hoisted my bag again and passed through the hall toward the kitchen, where the laundry machines were tucked in a closet. My sandy clothes would go directly into the wash; I always unpack within moments of returning from a trip. I turned the dial and sent hot water streaming loudly into the machine, then crossed to the refrigerator. Staring into this largely empty vault, I heard, over the water's rush, a faint thud. I straightened and glanced out the window. Through the blue evening murk, I saw the camper Robert hurrying across the overgrown back plot with a T-shirt slung around his neck and sneakers dangling from one hand. He lifted the latch on the rotting gate, slipped through and started to run down the alley barefoot, broken glass and all.

With a violent clunk, the washing machine swung into its agitation cycle. I crossed to it and began dropping the clothes into its maw piece by piece, staring as they were sucked into the vortex. I struggled to calm my quickening pulse, to get my spiraling dismay under control. Please, I said to myself, please. I sprinkled powder straight from the box, without measuring, and went to sit down in the darkening front room. I seemed to be sitting at the top of a steep slope; I clung to the sofa cushions with both hands. When Liss came out, her hair in a messy knot atop her head, and timidly suggested we order Chinese food for dinner, I said, "You do what you want." I thought about going to bed, to sleep, oblivion—but then an image of my daisy-festooned sheets, and of Liss and the boy tangled in them, passed sickeningly before my eyes, and I said, "I'm going to Barry's." He received me gladly, poured me a beer and allowed me my silence; I sat all evening slumped in an easy chair in his small study, watching him read, feeling my resolve to change things between us dissipating in the lamplight, like vapor.

At work the next day I was distracted from a major project—the dispensing of tens of millions to teachers of nutrition—by the thought of my sister luring a suicidal youth into her delinquent clutches. I had to stay late to get my tasks completed. The street was empty and full of shadows as I stumped up my block in new, badly fitting shoes. I happened to pass the van, parked in a dark gap between streetlamps, and something moving within it caught my eye. Cautiously, maintaining a distance of several feet, I peered inside. I saw a pair of thin shoulder blades, and a slowly waving foot, white and smooth as cheese. I backed away, pulse revving, and stumbled the rest of the way toward my door. I triple-locked it from the inside, and even engaged the little chain, my head buzzing, a sour drought taking hold in my mouth. In the kitchen I pulled the phone book from above the refrigerator. After a brief, urgent recitation of the alphabet's midsection I found the listing: "Loper, Blake," Fourth Street, Northeast. I dialed the number on the wall phone. A recorded voice answered, a man both businesslike and bashful. At the tone I hesitated and hung up.

In the back window was a reflection of the kitchen, with its fluorescent strip light over the sink. I stepped into the picture. My navy skirt flickered a mysterious plum purple

DEBRA JO IMMERGUT

in the reflection, and I saw I'd gone all day with my blouse
buttoned wrong. My eyes were hidden by light bouncing
off my glasses. I heard a key rattling the front door lock.
It stopped then started again, a skittery, trapped little
thing, trying and failing, trying and failing, to turn the
bolt. Then came a sharp yelp from the buzzer followed
by a rather soft knock on the heavy door, barely audible
from where I stood, frozen, staring at my image in the
kitchen window. Where would she go? I imagined the corner down by the Chicken Stop, where leering paper-bag
drinkers commented on passersby who dared cross their
litter-strewn turf. And then I thought of the skinny boy,
with his mouthful of braces. And of my mother's body
curled on the plaid daybed in the den. I bent over and
pulled off my shoes, exhausted, feeling decades older than
twenty-six.

In the living room, lit by the misty orange glow of the
anticrime streetlamps, I found Liss's vinyl suitcase stuffed
under the TV table. Her belongings were piled in a corner
of the room, behind a stereo speaker, where the carpet
succumbed to mildew every spring. The damp smell lin-
gered there, and mingled with the scent of Liss's clothes—a
faint mixture of summer sweat and baby powder. Pulling
a jersey from the top of the pile, I stuffed it into the bag,
then a pair of cut-off shorts and a tiny hardcover copy of
100 Love Poems. I grabbed another handful from behind
the speaker and yanked out a bundle of thinner cotton
garments. Even in the half-light, I instantly recognized
my mother's things—not just the gondola shorts were
there, but also the phases-of-the-moon pants, a panda-
bear-and-bamboo sleeveless top, and a skirt that cradled in
its folds memories of such intensity that I held its fine
weave to my face and burst into tears, squatting there in the
corner of my living room floor. The skirt was a silken
swirl she'd worn to milestone events in the 1970s, piano
recitals, grade-school graduations, chaperoning an eighth-

grade dance; and I remembered her dressed in it, heading out with my father on a Saturday night, watching from the front step as he opened the car door for her and waved good night to me. Its pearl-gray crepe was sprinkled with black-and-emerald sketches; from lyres to electric, it showed the whole history of guitars, and when she wore it I secretly shivered with pride at having a mother who was both with-it and demure.

A shattering of glass interrupted my bawling and I looked up, through tears, to see shards tumbling my way. I jerked backward and landed hard on my rump. Breaking my fall, my left hand came down on some glass, and I felt an edge slash the skin of my palm. I cursed loudly and brought the hand to my lap. I raised my eyes to the window. A wicked-looking hole, framed by glinting points, gaped in the lower pane. Liss's face, wide-eyed and dismayed, shone white in the void. "For Christ's sake, what are you doing?" I spat. She winced, seeing me, and lowered her eyes, holding the treacherous bulk of a holly shrub away from her face with one hand. "I was locked out," she said. She lifted her other hand and showed me a tire iron.

I snapped and turned the locks on the front door and swung it open for her, and in the white glare of the stoop light I saw that I'd stopped my hand's bleeding with the sacred guitar skirt, and that I'd bled quite a lot, and a large brick-red blotch stained the material just below the back waistband. As she emerged from the bushes with the tire iron in one hand and scratches on her bare legs, Liss said, "You were here?"

I waved the skirt. "Who gave you these clothes?"

"Ma gave them to me."

I stepped inside and she followed, shutting the door behind her. I crossed the living room to the pile of clothes and kicked it softly. "All her favorites?"

"Last summer she decided she wanted to wear only solids. Beige and black." With the edge of her sneaker, she started rounding up the larger slices of window glass. She looked up at me. "She went to a color consultant, and they told her that, black and beige." Something about the intimate way she gazed at me reminded me that my eyes and nose must've been red, tearsplotched. I held up my bloody palm and the skirt. "Look."

In the bathroom I found an Ace bandage from a time I'd sprained my ankle on the snowy steps of Monticello; I patted some toilet paper onto my palm and wrapped the bandage around my hand. I heard Liss go for the broom in the hall closet, and the small noises of the glass being swept up. I padded into my dark bedroom and sat on the unmade bed, my stiff bandaged hand resting next to my leg like a dead crab. "I'm sorry," I called. The broom's rustle stopped, and she yelled, "OK." A few ringing seconds of silence, then the sweeping started again. My arms and legs felt limp and loose. I thought about my mother in beige and black and it didn't seem right, not at all. But what do I know, I thought, staring hollow-hearted out the window at weeds swaying in the dark garden heat.

———

There are certain episodes of sexual misbehavior in the Rostow and Halloran histories. My Uncle Ted, Mom's only brother and a patriot who died on a peacetime mission in the Suez Canal, enlisted in the army after being fingered for a schoolmate's pregnancy. Grandma Halloran, perhaps to deflect attention from her son's transgression, told us shortly before she died that in 1949 a student had come to her in tears, distraught that her boss at Rostow's—old Opa himself—had offered her a hundred dollars for a hug—and she'd accepted it. "I told her to give the money to charity," Grandma said. And then there's my mother and the junior-high vice principal, Leff, witnessed passionately kissing in a downtown parking lot by a large group from Liss's ninth-grade class, who were waiting for a car pool home from dancing school. Needless to say, this brought Liss in for a good deal of ridicule. And worse, it was clear that Mom did not even like Leff so very much.

Liss comported herself admirably, putting a stop to her liaison. She couldn't bring herself to meet with Robert's father face-to-face, but she did speak with him at length on the phone, and it was finally agreed all around that if she gave up the Camp Victory job and promised never to contact the boy, no charges would be pressed.

That I could grant Liss a measure of my admiration only after the perpetration of two felonies (statutory rape is punishable by prison in every state and—Barry assured us—the application of tire iron to windowpane is forced entry even between sisters) is a fact of which I am not at all proud. I certainly wish it could have come about some better way. The plight of poor Robert is something that will needle me until I hear he's well-settled in a good job or marriage—and even after that I'll worry.

The day after she was dishonorably discharged from Camp Victory, on the first of August, a file-clerk slot in the library of Barry's firm happened to open up, and he offered to see what he could do. But Liss decided, and I did not disagree, that it might be best for her to return to Columbus and find a cheap student sublet in which to see the summer through. "They're easy to get," she said, "and you can rent them by the week." She took a tour of the Capitol building her last morning in town, and it was raining when we took her to the airport that afternoon, with an unsettling greenish light sifting down the western sky. Barry drove a new Japanese car he'd recently bought, and I sat beside him, with Liss in back. As we passed the Pentagon and its murky, moatlike lagoon, Liss leaned forward and said she'd left me the skirt with the guitars. "I thought you could fit into it better. That thing fit Mom only in her skinnier days."

"There's a big bloodstain on the back," I said.

"You can get it out with bleach." An arriving plane pressed down through the air above us and shot over the airport fence.

"Then it'll have a bleach stain on it."

"That's better than blood—right?" she said, and slid back on the seat. The rain spattered against the windows. She sighed. "Not a good day to fly."

"Actually," said Barry, glancing up at the sky, "pilots become more alert in bad weather."

We found a place in a pay lot, then crowded under my umbrella, threading toward the terminal between cars and oily puddles. Barry's remark still filled my ears, chiming there, words rolling; and now, days later, I am still hearing it. There is something so deeply comforting about that remark, I think—something so loving, so noble, so entirely good. When I watched him lift Liss's bag onto a passing redcap's cart, dark head bowed as he heaved the load up, I decided that a man who can think of such a thing to say is a man to be cherished, to be treasured. I furled the dripping umbrella and actually contemplated a life with him! Glass doors slid open, and I followed Barry, Liss, and the redcap into the building, hurrying dutifully behind as they snaked through the crowds, flushing businessmen from their path, dodging children.

DEBRA JO IMMERGUT was born in 1963 in Columbus, Ohio, grew up in Rockville and Potomac, Maryland, and attended the Universities of Michigan and Iowa. She is a recipient of a James A. Michener Fellowship and currently lives in Berlin, Germany. A collection of her stories is forthcoming in early 1992.

C. W. SMITH

WITNESSES

Norma should tell this story, but I don't think she will. So I have to do my best, though I might not tell it exactly as it happened. My story is this. Norma called me to say that her friend Patsy had died. I'd met Patsy once when she'd come to Dallas to collaborate with Norma on a book about quilting.

I told Norma I was sorry to hear about Patsy. "I know you must be devastated," I said. "You were friends for such a long time."

Yes, said Norma. "Since we were twelve." They'd grown up in New Mexico together, got married and divorced in tandem, stayed cross-continental pen pals for forty years. Patsy, childless, was godmother to Norma's daughter.

Was it cancer?

"Her heart exploded," said Norma.

You know Patsy, she went on, how she kept really fit and ran three miles a day—.

It was like Jim Fixx? No warning at all?

"Well, she'd had a leaky heart." A congenital condition. The doctors had told her she was at risk in jogging, "but she wanted to take care of her problem this way." And she'd been doing fine.

It happened while she was running?

No, it was like this. Patsy was coming out of a super-market. She was carrying a bag of groceries in her arms. A woman walking into the store happened to look at Patsy's face and saw her eyes roll back. She realized Patsy was passing out, so she stepped right up to Patsy and hugged her. The woman struggled to hold Patsy upright until a second woman, then a third, saw what was needed and rushed over to help the first woman lay Patsy back onto the floor. The second woman took off her gray cardigan, folded it, and slipped it under Patsy's head. While the third retrieved cans of cat food that had spilled from Patsy's sack, the first woman told a checker to call an ambulance. She pressed her fingers to Patsy's wrist but didn't feel a pulse. A fourth woman with wild red hair and paint-dabbed jeans went to her knees, loosened Patsy's concho belt, then blew into her mouth, over and over, and mas-saged her chest. Meanwhile, the second woman looked into Patsy's purse and located her home phone number, but when she went and called it, of course all she got was Patsy's machine. With nothing left to do, the other three knelt beside the woman doing CPR and waited.

The paramedics arrived but couldn't bring Patsy back. When they had put her on a stretcher and slid her into the ambulance, the first woman took out a business card, wrote on the back of it, and slipped it inside Patsy's purse, which the red-haired woman was holding. She in turn put the purse into the ambulance, and the third woman sat the groceries by Patsy's side.

———

The first woman's name is April Yuan, and she is a buyer for an import firm. When the ambulance left, she and the other three women stood at the curb for a minute, not knowing what to do. April Yuan had gone into the store to buy panty hose because she had a 2:30 meeting, and it was already three o'clock. The second woman draped her gray cardigan over her forearm and stroked it as you might a cat.

The other woman who had helped lay Patsy back, who had retrieved Patsy's cat food and had put Patsy's groceries in the ambulance, said, Well, I've got to go back to work now. It's a day-care center, couple blocks up that way. She looked to April Yuan and the others as if for permission to leave, and they shrugged and murmured that they understood. But then the day-care worker, a care-giver, made no move to go. The woman with the cardigan said, "I'm just visiting Berkeley, and I don't know anyone here." The woman who had tried CPR said, "I need to sit down and have some tea." The visitor with the cardigan looked relieved and said, "Me too."

They all four walked down the street a way until they came to a cafe none had ever been inside. The tables were of plywood with glossy, lacquered tops, and the menu said, We serve no caffeinated beverages. April Yuan, who has since been back to the place twice with Rachel, said the lunch crowd had cleared out. The place was quiet and empty but for one waitress who was wiping tables with a natural sponge the size of a bread loaf.

The four women ordered orange-cinnamon tea. The waitress brought a teapot with a blue glaze and four matching mugs on a tray. Then after a moment the waitress brought, unasked, fresh hot blueberry muffins for them to sample free. They didn't talk much at first. The red-haired woman lifted her mug high enough to peer at the bottom of it. Somebody said, "Poor woman." The visitor's hands were trembling, so her tea got cold before she could drink it. The red-haired woman said this was the only time she'd ever used her CPR training, and the others said don't feel bad—it was good that you tried, it was more than we did. The woman who worked at the day-care center asked, "I wonder if she had children?" April Yuan had noticed Patsy had no wedding ring.

They stayed for about an hour. The funny thing was, said April Yuan later, "We didn't talk about your friend Patsy very long." They didn't know what to say about what had happened. They all talked for a while about being parents and having them. The visitor with the cardigan said she had two teenage sons back home in Michigan. April Yuan has a grown daughter, but she told the others only about her mother, who has Alzheimer's. Then the visitor from Michigan asked the day-care woman how she put her hair in those corn rows. It takes days, answered the other. You got to wait until you want to punish yourself. They all laughed. They talked about the tea, the crockery. After a bit, April Yuan got up to go call her husband even though she knew he was busy at work, and when she came back to the table, the others were standing over the bill and chatting while they dug change out of their purses and pockets.

April was the last to leave the cafe. The woman with the teenage sons was already striding far up the street. A breeze had come up while they were in the cafe, and, while walking, the woman slipped her cardigan over her shoulders. Beside her, the day-care worker was gesturing in a way that meant giving directions. When the two reached the corner, they both looked back and waved good-bye. Then they disappeared.

The red-haired woman in the paint-smeared jeans had been lagging behind, letting the other two outpace her. She stopped and waited for April to catch up to her. "I'm Rachel," she said, and stuck out her hand. "I saw what you wrote on that card about being with her when she died. I hope someone from the family calls you."

Professor of English at Southern Methodist University, C. W. SMITH is the author of the novels *Thin Men of Haddam*, *Country Music*, *The Vestal Virgin Room*, and *Buffalo Nickel* and of the memoir *Uncle Dad*.

ELIZABETH WINTHROP

THE GOLDEN DARTERS

I was twelve years old
when my father started tying flies. It was an odd habit
for a man who had just undergone a serious operation on
his upper back, but, as he remarked to my mother one
night, at least it gave him a world over which he had some
control.

The family grew used to seeing him hunched down
close to his tying vise, hackle pliers in one hand, thread
bobbin in the other. We began to bandy about strange
phrases—foxy quills, bodkins, peacock hurl. Father's corner of the living room was off limits to the maid with
the voracious and destructive vacuum cleaner. Who knew
what precious bit of calf's tail or rabbit fur would be
sucked away never to be seen again.

Because of my father's illness, we had gone up to our
summer cottage on the lake in New Hampshire a month
early. None of my gang of friends ever came till the end of
July, so in the beginning of that summer I hung around
home watching my father as he fussed with the flies. I was
the only child he allowed to stand near him while he
worked. "Your brothers bounce," he muttered one day as
he clamped the vise onto the curve of a model-perfect
hook. "You can stay and watch if you don't bounce."

So I took great care not to bounce or lean or even breathe too noisily on him while he performed his delicate maneuvers, holding back hackle with one hand as he pulled off the final flourish of a whip finish with the other. I had never been so close to my father for so long before, and while he studied his tiny creations, I studied him. I stared at the large pores of his skin, the sleek black hair brushed straight back from the soft dip of his temples, the jaw muscles tightening and slackening. Something in my father seemed always to be ticking. He did not take well to sickness and enforced confinement.

When he leaned over his work, his shirt collar slipped down to reveal the recent scar, a jagged trail of disrupted tissue. The tender pink skin gradually paled and then toughened during those weeks when he took his prescribed afternoon nap, lying on his stomach on our little patch of front lawn. Our house was one of the closest to the lake and it seemed to embarrass my mother to have him stretch himself out on the grass for all the swimmers and boaters to see.

"At least sleep on the porch," she would say. "That's why we set the hammock up there."

"Why shouldn't a man sleep on his own front lawn if he so chooses?" he would reply. "I have to mow the bloody thing. I might as well put it to some use."

And my mother would shrug and give up.

At the table when he was absorbed, he lost all sense of anything but the magnified insect under the light. Often when he pushed his chair back and announced the completion of his latest project to the family, there would be a bit of down or a tuft of dubbing stuck to the edge of his lip. I did not tell him about it but stared, fascinated, wondering how long it would take to blow away. Sometimes it never did and I imagine he discovered the fluff in the bathroom mirror when he went upstairs to bed. Or maybe my mother plucked it off with one of those proprietary gestures of hers that irritated my brothers so much.

In the beginning, Father wasn't very good at the fly-tying. He was a large, thickboned man with sweeping gestures, a robust laugh, and a sudden terrifying temper. If he had not loved fishing so much, I doubt he would have persevered with the fussy business of the flies. After all, the job required tools normally associated with woman's work. Thread and bobbins, soft slippery feathers, a magnifying glass, and an instruction manual that read like a cookbook. It said things like, "Cut off a bunch of yellow-tail. Hold the tip end with the left hand and stroke out the short hairs."

But Father must have had a goal in mind. You tie flies because one day, in the not-too-distant future, you will attach them to a tippet, wade into a stream, and lure a rainbow trout out of his quiet pool.

There was something endearing, almost childish, about his stubborn nightly ritual at the corner table. His head bent under the standing lamp, his fingers trembling slightly, he would whisper encouragement to himself, talk his way through some particularly delicate operation. Once or twice I caught my mother gazing silently across my brothers' heads at him. When our eyes met, she would turn away and busy herself in the kitchen.

Finally, one night, after weeks of allowing me to watch, he told me to take his seat. "Why, Father?"

"Because it's time for you to try one."

"That's all right. I like to watch."

"Nonsense, Emily. You'll do just fine."

He had stood up. The chair was waiting. Across the room, my mother put down her knitting. Even the boys, embroiled in a noisy game of double solitaire, stopped their wrangling for a moment. They were all waiting to see what I would do. It was my fear of failing him that made me hesitate. I knew that my father put his trust in results, not in the learning process.

"Sit down, Emily."

I obeyed, my heart pounding. I was a cautious, secretive child, and I could not bear to have people watch me doing things. My piano lesson was the hardest hour in the week. The teacher would sit with a resigned look on her face while my fingers groped across the keys, muddling through a sonata that I had played perfectly just an hour before. The difference was that then nobody had been watching.

"—so we'll start you off with a big hook." He had been talking for some time. How much had I missed already?

"Ready?" he asked.

I nodded.

"All right then, clamp this hook into the vise. You'll be making the golden darter, a streamer. A big flashy fly, the kind that imitates a small fish as it moves underwater."

Across the room, my brothers had returned to their game but their voices were subdued. I imagined they wanted to hear what was happening to me. My mother had left the room.

"Tilt the magnifying glass so you have a good view of the hook. Right. Now tie on with the bobbin thread."

It took me three tries to line the thread up properly on the hook, each silken line nesting next to its neighbor. "We're going to do it right, Emily, no matter how long it takes."

"It's hard," I said quietly.

Slowly I grew used to the tiny tools, to the oddly enlarged view of my fingers through the magnifying glass. They looked as if they didn't belong to me anymore. The feeling in their tips was too small for their large, clumsy movements. Despite my father's repeated warnings, I nicked the floss once against the barbed hook. Luckily it did not give way.

"It's Emily's bedtime," my mother called from the kitchen.

"Hush, she's tying in the throat. Don't bother us now."

I could feel his breath on my neck. The mallard barbules were stubborn, curling into the hook in the wrong direction. Behind me, I sensed my father's fingers twisting in imitation of my own.

"You've almost got it," he whispered, his lips barely moving. "That's right. Keep the thread slack until you're all the way around."

I must have tightened it too quickly. I lost control of the feathers in my left hand, the clumsier one. First the gold mylar came unwound and then the yellow floss.

"Damn it all, now look what you've done," he roared, and for a second I wondered whether he was talking to me. He sounded as if he were talking to a grown-up. He sounded the way he had just the night before when an antique teacup had slipped through my mother's soapy fingers and shattered against the hard surface of the sink. I sat back slowly, resting my aching spine against the chair for the first time since we'd begun.

"Leave it for now, Gerald," my mother said tentatively from the kitchen. Out of the corner of my eye, I could see her sponging the kitchen counter with small, defiant sweeps of her hand. "She can try again tomorrow."

"What happened?" called a brother. They both started across the room toward us but stopped at a look from my father.

"We'll start again," he said, his voice once more under control. "Best way to learn. Get back on the horse."

With a flick of his hand, he loosened the vise, removed my hook, and threw it into the wastepaper basket.

"From the beginning?" I whispered.

"Of course," he replied. "There's no way to rescue a mess like that."

My mess had taken almost an hour to create.

"Gerald," my mother said again. "Don't you think—"

"How can we possibly work with all these interruptions?" he thundered. I flinched as if he had hit me. "Go on upstairs, all of you. Emily and I will be up when we're done. Go on, for God's sake. Stop staring at us."

At a signal from my mother, the boys backed slowly away and crept up to their room. She followed them. I felt all alone, as trapped under my father's piercing gaze as the hook in the grip of its vise.

We started again. This time my fingers were trembling so much that I ruined three badger hackle feathers, stripping off the useless webbing at the tip. My father did not lose his temper again. His voice dropped to an even, controlled monotone that scared me more than his shouting. After an hour of painstaking labor, we reached the same point with the stubborn mallard feathers curling into the hook. Once, twice, I repinched them under the throat, but each time they slipped away from me. Without a word, my father stood up and leaned over me. With his cheek pressed against my hair, he reached both hands around and took my fingers in his. I longed to surrender the tools to him and slide away off the chair, but we were so close to the end. He captured the curling stem with the thread and trapped it in place with three quick wraps.

"Take your hands away carefully," he said. "I'll do the whip finish. We don't want to risk losing it now."

I did as I was told, sat motionless with his arms around me, my head tilted slightly to the side so he could have the clear view through the magnifying glass. He cemented the head, wiped the excess glue from the eye with a waste feather, and hung my golden darter on the tackle-box handle to dry. When at last he pulled away, I breathlessly slid my body back against the chair. I was still conscious of the havoc my clumsy hands or an unexpected sneeze could wreak on the table which was cluttered with feathers and bits of fur.

"Now, that's the fly you tied, Emily. Isn't it beautiful?"
I nodded. "Yes, Father."

"Tomorrow, we'll do another one. An olive grouse. Smaller hook but much less complicated body. Look. I'll show you in the book."

As I waited to be released from the chair, I didn't think he meant it. He was just trying to apologize for having lost his temper, I told myself, just trying to pretend that our time together had been wonderful. But the next morning when I came down, late for breakfast, he was waiting for me with the materials for the olive grouse already assembled. He was ready to start in again, to take charge of my clumsy fingers with his voice and talk them through the steps.

That first time was the worst, but I never felt comfortable at the fly-tying table with Father's breath tickling the hair on my neck. I completed the olive grouse, another golden darter to match the first, two muddler minnows and some others. I don't remember all the names anymore.

Once I hid upstairs, pretending to be immersed in my summer reading books, but he came looking for me.

"Emily," he called. "Come on down. Today we'll start the leadwinged coachman. I've got everything set up for you."

I lay very still and did not answer.

"Gerald," I heard my mother say. "Leave the child alone. You're driving her crazy with those flies."

"Nonsense," he said and started up the dark, wooden stairs, one heavy step at a time.

I put my book down and rolled slowly off the bed so that by the time he reached the door of my room, I was on my feet, ready to be led back downstairs to the table.

Although we never spoke about it, my mother became oddly insistent that I join her on trips to the library or the general store.

"Are you going out again, Emily?" my father would call

after me. "I was hoping we'd get some work done on this minnow."

"I'll be back soon, Father," I'd say. "I promise."

"Be sure you do," he said.

And for a while I did.

———

Then at the end of July, my old crowd of friends from across the lake began to gather and I slipped away to join them early in the morning before my father got up.

The girls were a gang. When we were all younger, we'd held bicycle relay races on the ring road and played down at the lakeside together under the watchful eyes of our mothers. Every July, we threw ourselves joyfully back into each other's lives. That summer we talked about boys and smoked illicit cigarettes in Randy Kidd's basement and held leg-shaving parties in her bedroom behind a safely locked door. Randy was the ringleader. She was the one who suggested we pierce our ears.

"My parents would die," I said. "They told me I'm not allowed to pierce my ears until I'm seventeen."

"Your hair's so long, they won't even notice," Randy said. "My sister will do it for us. She pierces all her friends' ears at college."

In the end, only one girl pulled out. The rest of us sat in a row with the obligatory ice cubes held to our ears waiting for the painful stab of the sterilized needle.

Randy was right. At first my parents didn't notice. Even when my ears became infected, I didn't tell them. All alone in my room, I went through the painful procedure of twisting the gold studs and swabbing the recent wounds with alcohol. Then on the night of the club dance, when I had changed my clothes three times and played with my hair in front of the mirror for hours, I came across the small plastic box with dividers in my top bureau drawer. My father had given it to me so that I could keep my flies in separate compartments, untangled from one another. I poked my finger in and slid one of the golden darters up along its plastic wall. When I held it up, the mylar thread sparkled in the light like a jewel. I took out the other darter, hammered down the barbs of the two hooks, and slipped them into the raw holes in my earlobes.

Someone's mother drove us all to the dance, and Randy and I pushed through the side door into the ladies' room. I put my hair up in a ponytail so the feathered flies could twist and dangle above my shoulders. I liked the way they made me look—free and different and dangerous even. And they made Randy notice.

"I've never seen earrings like that," Randy said. "Where did you get them?"

"I made them with my father. They're flies. You know, for fishing."

"They're great. Can you make me some?"

I hesitated. "I have some others at home I can give you," I said at last. "They're in a box in my bureau."

"Can you give them to me tomorrow?" she asked.

"Sure," I said with a smile. Randy had never noticed anything I'd worn before. I went out to the dance floor, swinging my ponytail in time to the music.

———

My mother noticed the earrings as soon as I got home.

"What has gotten into you, Emily? You know you were forbidden to pierce your ears until you were in college. This is appalling."

I didn't answer. My father was sitting in his chair behind the fly-tying table. His back was better by that time, but he still spent most of his waking hours in that chair. It was as if he didn't like to be too far away from his flies, as if something might blow away if he weren't keeping watch.

I saw him look up when my mother started in with me. His hands drifted ever so slowly down to the surface of the table as I came across the room toward him. I leaned over so that he could see my earrings better in the light.

"Everybody loved them, Father. Randy says she wants a pair, too. I'm going to give her the muddler minnows."

"I can't believe you did this, Emily," my mother said in a loud, nervous voice. "It makes you look so cheap."

"They don't make me look cheap, do they, Father?" I swung my head so he could see how they bounced, and my hip accidentally brushed the table. A bit of rabbit fur floated up from its pile and hung in the air for a moment before it settled down on top of the foxy quills.

"For God's sake, Gerald, speak to her," my mother said from her corner.

He stared at me for a long moment as if he didn't know who I was anymore, as if I were a trusted associate who had committed some treacherous and unspeakable act. "That is not the purpose for which the flies were intended," he said.

"Oh, I know that," I said quickly. "But they look good this way, don't they?"

He stood up and considered me in silence for a long time across the top of the table lamp.

"No, they don't," he finally said. "They're hanging upside down."

Then he turned off the light and I couldn't see his face anymore.

ELIZABETH WINTHROP grew up in Washington, D.C., and is the author of *In My Mother's House* as well as more than thirty books for children. Ms. Winthrop lives in New York City.

American Short Fiction

HELENS AND ROSES

he minute the job was done and the man drove away, leaving the trailer windows covered with toast-colored blinds drawn tight as Dick's hatband, Pep started complaining. "You can't hardly tell if it's daylight or dark since you put up these curtains."

"Blinds," Lula said, already feeling the difference they made. The cost, of course, had knocked her flat. But she'd long ago learned what you want in this world you have to pay for, and she wanted those blinds, more than new chairs or an air conditioner.

"What for?" Pep said when she brought up the subject the first time around.

"We need them," she said. She couldn't explain the pure-d fright of night coming on since they moved into town, of the dark reaching out from the houses and streets. From she didn't know where. "We need the protection," was what she told Pep.

"What I need is air," Pep said now. "Let's raise the things up."

"We just put 'em down." Lula walked back and forth, admiring the blinds. The toast color was right. It lifted the gloom of the mud-colored walls and made the rooms airy. "Stretch out on the couch if your head is hurting."

"What hurts is to think what that bozo charged."

"No more than they're worth. They dress up the place."

"Your teacups do that—and they don't stop the breeze."

The first time the man came, he came on a Thursday, one of Pep's bad days. He brought his dog. Then he started right in with how hot it was, how he'd have to step out and see about Sheri out in the van.

"Scheherazade," Lula said to Pep, back in the bedroom where he'd gone to lie down. "That's the name of the dog."

"There's a dog in the house?" His blue eyes opened. Pep missed Prince Rudy, the best hound of his life that he'd had to sell off on account of the rule Lula had made, *No dogs in town,* when they moved from the Sandies. *They can't run loose, and they sure as the dickens aren't coming inside.*

"She's out in the van," Lula said. "Sheri, he calls her."

"Who? His wife? Why don't she come in?" Pep got off the track when his head acted up. Sometimes just a minute. Or maybe all day, the way it was lately.

As a general rule, though, they did pretty well. They lived clean lives, Pep liked to say, and except for his mix-ups, his mind stayed clear. Clearer than hers, Lula claimed. He could tell you dates way back to the Flood, even days of the week when certain things happened, especially his dog deals, like trading the setter in '38 to Pinky McClure for a broad-nosed sow and a couple of shoats. (On a Tuesday that happened—a May afternoon right after a shower.)

"Lie there and rest," Lula said that Thursday. "When he comes back here, you can move to the front."

Lula herself had varicose veins. And hemorrhoids at night. Let her turn on her back and they started in throbbing. She had learned a trick, though—to bear down for a minute, not too hard—and the pain went away. That's all there was to it, a few minutes of pressure. Gravity, she guessed it was. Out of the blue, she knew how to do it.

"What's he coming back here for?"

"To measure the windows."

"Why?" Pep said.

"For the blinds. I told you."

The next time the man came he brought the blinds with him. He left the dog in the yard, tied to a tree. She ran all around it, yipping and yapping.

"She's a nervous animal," Lula said.

"Yes, ma'am," said the man. "Spoiled rotten." He looked spoiled himself, Lula thought. He had a loose kind of look around his mouth and watery eyes set close to his nose. "She belongs with my wife, but my wife's with our daughter. In Panama City."

"Where the dictator is?"

"In Florida, ma'am. How is your husband?"

"He's all right today. He'll be out in a minute."

The man stood on a footstool. "It's the heat, I suppose, that gives him those headaches."

"Pep's ninety, you know."

"He sure doesn't look it."

"I'm eighty-two."

"You don't look it either."

Pep said again, "Let's put up the shades."

"It's nighttime, Dad."

Dad was only a name. They never had children. Never wanted them much, Pep had told his brother, which wasn't the truth. They hoped for two. Pep wanted twins. They had to fill up their lives in place of those children. Pep took up dogs. Lula settled on teacups and various things.

They were younger, of course, up on the Sandies, a little dry creek that could rise when it wanted but mostly ran quiet, bedded in sand with a few brown pools that a fish or two slept in.

They were there fifty years. Then they moved into town.

Their trailer just fit on a sliver of land next to the Quik-Stop, down a little, with a hedge in between, but the lights from the cars swept in at all hours, giving Lula the jitters.

"Like spotlights," she said. "Like they're hunting us down." She mentioned the blinds.

Pep voted for shades. "They come a lot cheaper."

"With blinds," Lula said, "you can tilt in the light and still have your privacy."

The day the man hung them he gave her some tips about which way to turn them.

"Most people get it backwards. They turn the slats down." He was sweating by then. "But let's say, for example, there's a peeper outside."

It gave Lula a chill to think that there might be.

"With the slats tilted down they look like they're closed, but out where he's at, he gets the whole picture."

He sent Lula outside to prove he was right.

She told this to Pep, helping him dress. "He sure knows his business."

Pep wound his watch. "Has he brought in the dog?"

"He brought her up the steps and gave her some water. She's roped to the tree, a little fluffy orange pooch." Lula hunted her glasses, first on the dresser and then in the bathroom.

"You're wearing the things," Pep pointed out.

"For goodness sakes." Lula pushed up the nosepiece. "She's an apricot poodle."

"I know what she is. I can't think what he calls her."

"Scheherazade."

"Spell it," said Pep. He was hell on spelling. He once won a meet and was given a ribbon. "CHAMPEEN," it said. Lula laughed when he showed her. A spelling prize and they spelled it wrong.

"It starts with an *s,* that's all I know." But then she went on. "It's the name of that woman who kept telling stories to stay alive. In *Arabian Nights.*"

"A picture show?"

"A book when I read it. I had it in school."

School for Lula was out on the prairie. White Hall it was called. The teacher there was Miss Mabel Barnes, on her way up as an educator. She made it, in fact, to County Superintendent, and on from there right into Houston. At White Hall her mission was to introduce culture.

"There are children out here that don't know a fairy tale from Adam's off ox." She was a little pale woman, born to a doctor that lived in Fort Worth when there weren't many such—female doctors.

Lula took to culture, the myths most especially, how things got like they were, why spiders make webs, that kind of thing.

Education stays with you, is what Lula said.

Viewing the blinds, she said to Pep, "I feel a lot safer."

"Safer from what?" Up on the Sandies she was scareder of june bugs than she was of the wolves. Moths gave her a tizzy, the big hairy kind that flew in the window.

Pep, however, liked all things in nature. He liked to lie in the bed with the wind on his face and listen to owls. He had talked to a fellow over at the Quik-Stop that didn't even know owls made a whooping sound. "Like a cowboy yelling *yippy-ti-yo.*"

"Owls hoot," the man said.

"Well, sure they do." Pep followed him out and poked his head in the car. "But they have a cry, too."

The man drove away. "Damn city fool," Pep said to Lula.

"Safe from criminals," Lula said.

Pep snorted at that. "Do you think you'll get murdered in this sleepy burg?" He had visited great cities. He once went to sea.

"It happens all over." In Lula's nightmares, crooks knocked down the door.

It wasn't much of a door, they both agreed. When they first came to town to size up the trailer—a sleek cream and beige with a bowed-out front where Pep stretched the flag—he put into words what was holding him back. "It's too smooth inside."

It was, Lula saw. A toy kind of outfit. When you knocked on a wall it didn't sound solid. It sounded, Pep said, like a cereal box.

They bought it anyway, with most of their capital. They were too old for loans is what it boiled down to. And too old for the country. What if one of them died?

When Lula met Pep she was barely fourteen. She had her hair in a net, no shoes on her feet, and was cleaning a skillet from fish she had fried that had stuck like glue. She was out by the barn and he came riding up on a no-count horse.

He was looking for cows. This was up on the Sandies where later they settled. There was brush all around with cow paths through it and lots of wild roses in hedges so thick you could bleed to death if you hung up in one and tried in a hurry to get yourself loose.

He came out of the yaupon, all dressed up on that pitiful pony, his legs hanging down almost to the ground.

"Nice morning," he said and tipped his hat.

She knew who he was from the dent in his chin and his sky-colored eyes. Her sister had told her. "You're Pepper McLeod."

He inclined his gaze to her feet in the dust. "You're the Bennett girl with the beautiful toes."

She covered them up under chicken-scratched earth. "What are you doing way off over here?"

"They told me in town to hurry on out before you got married."

"Aw, git on." But she half-believed he meant what he said.

He got off his horse. "Let me have that skillet." He went to the trough and dipped it in. "Now give me the rag."

He hung around for a while. He asked her age. She told him sixteen and changed the subject. "Do you always go riding in Sunday clothes?"

"When I'm out meeting girls."

She guessed that was true. He had girls all over, her sister said.

Then the cows came along, mooing and lowing, and gathered around him. "Here the girls are now."

She couldn't help laughing. He got back on his horse, laughing too. "Do you ever go dancing?"

"Of course," she lied. "When I want to, I do."

"How often is that?"

"When you see me you'll know."

He lifted his hat and gave her the look her sister had told her made girls pitch over and faint in the road. "Good-bye, Lula Bennett."

She loved him already. "Good-bye, Pep McLeod."

He didn't come back. He forgot her, she guessed.

In the time he was gone she got a lot older. She broke her wrist cranking a car. She bobbed her hair, got thin in the waist, bought a pair of kid gloves, and spent money on dresses that should have gone to the church.

She was working by then on a telephone switchboard and going out with men who bragged on her looks and asked her to marry them. One owned a saloon and a domino parlor and drove a Ford car the top went down on. Emmit Steele he was named, for his father the barber. He bought her a ring, but she wouldn't wear it. She said maybe she might if the sign got right.

Her sister got married. Her father died. Her mother moved off from the place on the Sandies.

Lula went there one day and found a black snake asleep in a chair. In the room that was hers, birds lay on their backs with their feet in the air.

Emmit Steele was along. "Let's get out of here."

"Wait," Lula said. She went to the window and looked

at the horse trough where Pepper McLeod had scrubbed her skillet. She made up her mind. If he didn't come back she would never get married. She would stay an old maid and have put on her tombstone *Born and Died* and not a thing else.

———

While the man hung the blinds Lula went to the store. Not to the Quik-Stop. She went in the car. First she took off the bedspread she covered it with to keep off the cats. Then she backed it slowly into the street.

Pep said to the man, "You could bring in your dog and let her cool off."

"She's fine outside." His name was Winkle.

"These delicate dogs keel over and die."

Winkle peered toward the yard.

"Go on with your work. I'll go out and fetch her."

Lula browsed in the store. When Pep was along she had to shop fast. He bought the wrong things. He bought everything big, the biggest bananas, big boxes of crackers that always went stale.

He was married before. Briefly, to women named Helen and Rose. One was a teacher who died right away, and the other one, Rose, fell out of love.

Lula didn't know this when Pep came back. He took her out a few times and then he said, "The day Helen died—"

"Helen who?" she asked.

About Rose he said, "We married for fun."

She took it slow after that. She went out again with Emmit Steele, and a new butcher in town who sang in the choir.

Pep seemed not to mind. He met her one day by the bank on the corner. "Whenever you're ready, say the word."

She was wearing new shoes with buckles that glittered. "Ready for what?"

"To be my wife."

"Wife Number 3?"

"We'll do all right. We'll make a good pair."

"Hah," she said, "you don't respect women."

"I do." He was hurt. "I have sisters," he said.

Pep sat on the couch and drew Winkle out. "What else have you done besides hanging blinds?" He fed Sheri a cookie, a gingersnap.

"I've raced horses," said Winkle, pleased to be asked.

"My business is dogs. What'll you take for Scheherazade?"

"Oh," Winkle said, "she's not for sale. She belongs to my wife."

Pep pulled on his chin. "She's got a bum leg. You'd have to whittle your price."

"There's no way I'd sell her."

"Because of your wife." Pep studied a minute on Winkle's wife. He pictured her tall, with a downy mustache. She wore suits, he thought, and had a long neck and ears that lay back, like a panther's ears.

"Winkle," said Pep, "I'm a breeder, too. We could make us some money, depending, of course, on what ails the leg."

When Lula came home she knew right away the dog had come in. She took Pep aside.

"Sheri's been in the house."

"What makes you think so?"

"Crumbs on the rug. And I smell her perfume."

"Perfume on a dog?"

"There are people that silly."

"I'm glad I was shaving."

"You should have watched out."

———

When they moved into town Lula put up her teacups. Not out for display, but in boxes she stored in the two bedroom closets.

They had always sat out and Pep found he missed them, the main one especially, from Miss Mabel Barnes. A plain green cup with President Wilson in black on the side.

"The trailer's too wobbly," Lula said. "They'd fall down and break."

"What good are they doing shut up in the dark?"

"I don't want to dust them."

Pep made her sit down. "I don't think that's it."

Lula twitched in her chair. "What's the matter with you?"

He gave her the look girls had swooned in the dust for. "You gave up your cups because I can't have my dogs."

"You're the beatingest man."

"I'm right, aren't I, Lu?"

He built shelves all around and helped her unpack them. "We're fixed up now."

"All but Prince Rudy."

"Rudy," said Pep, "wouldn't like it in town."

Lula held out her arms. "Would you care to dance?"

Up on the Sandies they always went dancing. Forty miles to a dance hall was nothing at all. Except once for six weeks when Pep had pleurisy. It hurt even to walk. "It sears my chest."

He was something to scare you, a big strong man and he couldn't get up. Lula hovered around. "You ought to get out. You ought to breathe in some Vicks."

"That'd sure enough kill me." He expected to die and made plans for Lula. "You could get you a job in a cafe or something."

"I'd work on a switchboard," she said, insulted.

"They've gone out of style."

"Who says so?" said Lula.

"They've gone to the dial."

She sat down and cried for all she had lost, for marrying Pep who was sick all the time, and a barren womb, and the holes in her stockings.

"Come here, little girl."

She wouldn't go near him. "Get up from the bed! And don't talk of dying."

He talked about girls. There were more than she knew of, scattered around. Even some overseas. Alice in England. And Fleurette and Marie. He forgot where they came from. "Two really nice girls."

Lula threw the green cup and gave President Wilson a crack in his glasses. Patching him up with flour-paste glue, Pep commented mildly, "It's you that I married."

"The third on the list." She was sobbing still.

"You would have been first if you'd been a day older."

———

Pep went to sea on the *Tarkington Trader*. A saber ship is what it was called, for the way it cut water.

It happened right funny how he got on.

He was wasting his life, his father said—a serious man who owned two ranches and had other sons that tended to business. This one he saw as a ne'er-do-well.

"What'll it take to straighten you out?"

Pep knew right away. "Five hundred dollars." He wanted a car to drive people around, land men he'd met who came in on trains from Northern cities and couldn't get out to look at the prairies.

His father thought girls was what he was after. "You won't get it from me. Get out and earn it."

"Two-fifty?" tried Pep. He'd saved ninety himself. For two-forty more he could buy a Tin Lizzie.

"Not twenty-five cents," his father told him.

"Then I'm leaving the country," Pepper said.

He tried Mexico first and liked it fine, except for warm goat's milk and breakfast menudo—and the way they slit throats over practically nothing. He got out fast one night in September and went up to Corpus and hid on a ship.

"The damned thing sailed." He laughed, telling Lula.

She remembered those days when she waited, forgotten. "You were gone a long time."

"Four years on the sea."

"And two wives later."

Helen died in a dentist's chair, having a tooth pulled. About Rose, Pep said: "Rose? She was pretty."

"Let's have some air," he insisted again.

"I'll fan you," said Lula, and took up *The Post*.

The women Pep married she dwelt on in bed. At other times, too. She had in her mind delicate Helen and beautiful Rose while she stood canning pears that came off the trees that bloomed on the Sandies like lace-adorned brides.

She was married herself in a preacher's front room, wearing navy blue and a hat on her head. Then they got in Pep's truck with a hound in the back and went up on the creek and settled in.

"I know about pain, Pep. I know how to stop it."

"It's not pain exactly."

"What is it then?"

He never could tell her. "Like a fog," he explained. "Like a bag on my head. Like I don't know my name."

"You bear down," Lula said. "In a minute, it's gone."

"Bear down on my head?"

"There's another way, too." She hated to tell him because it was hard, even for her (and she was all for it). "You pinpoint the pain. You search it out with a finger of thought."

"A finger of what?"

"You concentrate, Pep. You bear down with your mind on finding the pain at the place where it starts. *Is it here?* you ask. *Is this where it is?* Wherever your mind goes, the pain disappears."

"Lu," he said, "will you bring me the aspirins?"

For a living, he farmed, a handful of acres he cleared with a mule. When he had extra cash he bet on the cock fights. He made money with dogs, but they never had water that ran from a pipe, or electric power, till they moved into town.

Pep told Lula once that Emmit Steele had got rich, driving land men all over creation. "But he hasn't had fun. He hasn't had you."

"Sit up," Lula said, "and swallow these tablets." Pep gurgled them down. She thought of the day she stood at the window and vowed not to marry any man except this one. "Are you all right now?"

"Tell me a story. One of those myths."

"Scheherazade?"

"I don't care what it is."

Lula thought back to White Hall. "She married a man that was killing his wives. She had to keep telling tales till she finally saved him."

"The woman saved *him?*"

"From his murderous ways."

Pep gave a chuckle. "You tangle things up, Lu. You don't know the truth."

"Maybe I don't."

He dropped off to sleep. Then he woke up and said, "You never have known my true feelings for women."

"Hah," Lula said, "I ought to have known."

"I've been drawn to 'em somehow."

"I guess I know *that.*"

"Like a bee drawn to flowers."

"To Helens and Roses."

"Not to their bodies." He reached out and pinched her. "Except for yours. It's what makes them go, that was what pulled me."

"Eyes were what pulled you, and thick, curly hair."

"Ah, Lula, no. What I like is to watch 'em, to watch how they do. Women," he said, "are a curiosity."

Lula saw all at once that a shiver had seized him. "Are you getting too cool?" She stopped swinging *The Post.*

"No, go on."

"Go on with what?"

"Talk," he said. "It eases my head."

"Where was I?" she asked.

He couldn't quite answer. He thought he heard owls, not their cowboy cries, but the soft feathery sounds the mice probably heard and then went into trances.

"Pep?" Lula said.

He lay very still on the rim of his name and saw in the water what amounted to fish with silver-blue sides. A long time ago he had dreamed of such fish, dreamed he had caught them with only his hands.

"You're dozing," said Lula. "Pep, are you dozing?"

She watched for his breath, for the lift of his shirt or some kind of motion. "I can raise up the blind."

She pulled on the cord and the darkness rushed in with sounds from the Quik-Stop, quick feet on the pavement.

"That man let his dog in, let her up on the couch." She circled around. "That bow in her hair and her toenails painted. But I guess it's all right. She didn't have fleas." Prince Rudy had fleas. All of his ancestors leaped with fleas.

She sat down all at once and took hold of Pep's hand. "Can you see the cabin? The swing on the porch and the moon coming up with the dogs at our feet?" She started to cry then. "Remember the dancing?"

Finally she said, when the noise at the Quik-Stop had stopped altogether, "Pep, can you hear me?" She faltered a bit and then found her voice. "Up on the Sandies we never had night. We had a long spell of light." Through her eyelids she saw it: long golden light that lasted and lasted. ⌇

ANNETTE SANFORD was born in Cuero, Texas. She is the author of 25 paperback romances published under five pseudonyms, and of numerous short stories, written under her own name. *Lasting Attachments,* a collection of these stories, was published recently. She lives with her husband, Lukey, in Ganado, Texas, where she taught high-school English for twenty-five years before she turned to writing full time.

BARRY LOPEZ

REMEMBERING ORCHARDS

*J*n the years I lived with my stepfather
I didn't understand his life at all. He and my mother married when I was twelve, and by the time I was seventeen I
had gone away to college. I had little contact with him after
that until, oddly, just before he died, when I was twenty-
six. Now, years later, my heart grows silent, thinking of
what I gave up by maintaining my differences with him.

He was a farmer and an orchardist, and in these skills a
man of the first rank. By the time we met, my head was full
of a desire to travel, to find work like my friends in a place
far from the farming country where I was raised. My father and mother had divorced violently; this second marriage, I now realize, was not just calm but serene. Rich. Another part of my shame is that I forfeited this knowledge,
too. Conceivably, it was something I could have spoken to
him about in my early twenties, during my first marriage.

It is filbert orchards that have brought him back to me.
I am a printer. I live in a valley in western Oregon, along
a river where there are filbert orchards. Just on the other
side of the mountains, not so far away, are apple and pear
orchards of great renown. I have taken from these trees,
from their arrangement over the ground and from my curiosity about them in the different seasons, a peace I cannot

readily understand. It has, I know, to do with him, with the way his hands went fearlessly to the bark of the trees as he pruned late in the fall. Even I, who held him vaguely in contempt, could not miss the kindness, the sensuousness of these gestures.

Our home was in Granada Hills in California, a little more than forty acres of trees and gardens which my stepfather tended with the help of a man from Ensenada I regarded as more sophisticated at the time. Ramón Castillo was in his twenties, always with a new girlfriend clinging passionately to him, and able to make anything grow voluptuously in the garden, working with an aplomb that bordered on disdain.

The orchards—perhaps this is too strong an image, but it is nevertheless exactly how I felt—represented in my mind primitive creatures in servitude. The orchards were like penal colonies to me. I saw nothing but the rigid order of the plat, the harvesting, the pruning, the mechanics of it ultimately. I missed my stepfather's affection, understood it only as pride or gratification, missed entirely his humility.

Where I live now I have been observing orchards along the river, and over these months, or perhaps years, of watching, it has occurred to me that my stepfather responded most deeply not to the orchard's neat and systematic regimentation, to the tasks of maintenance associated with that, but to a chaos beneath. What I saw as productive order he saw as a vivid surface of exquisite tension. The trees were like sparrows frozen in flight, their single identities overshadowed by the insistent precision of the whole. Internal heresy—errant limbs, minor inconsistencies in spacing or height—was masked by stillness.

I have, within my boyhood memories, many images of these orchards, and of neighboring groves and orchards on other farms at the foot of the Santa Susanas. But I had a point of view that was common, uninspired. I could imagine the trees as prisoners, but I could not imagine them as transcendent, living in a time and on a plane inaccessible to me.

When I left the farm I missed the trees no more than my chores.

———

The insipid dimension of my thoughts became apparent years later, on two successive days after two very mundane observations. The first day, a still winter afternoon—I remember I had just finished setting type for an installment of Olsen's *Maximus Poems,* an arduous task, and was driving to town—I looked beneath the hanging shower of light-green catkins, just a glance under the roof-crown of a thousand filbert trees, to see one branch fallen from a jet-black trunk onto fresh snow. It was just a moment, as the road swooped away and I with it.

The second day I drove more slowly past the same spot and saw a large flock of black crows walking over the snow, all spread out, their graceless strides. I thought not of death, the usual flat images in that cold silence, but of Ramón Castillo. One night I saw him twenty rows deep in the almond orchard, my eye drawn in by moonlight brilliant on his white shorts. He stood gazing at the stars. A woman lay on her side at his feet, turned away, perhaps asleep. The trees in that moment seem not to exist, to be a field of indifferent posts. As the crows strode diagonally through the orchard rows I thought of the single broken branch hanging down, and of Ramón's ineffable solitude, and I saw the trees like all life—incandescent, pervasive.

In that moment I felt like an animal suddenly given its head.

———

My stepfather seemed to me, when I was young, too polite a man to admire. There was nothing forceful about him at a time when I admired obsession. He was lithe, his movement very physical but gentle, distinct, and hard to forget. The Chinese say of the contrast in such strength and fluidity, "movement like silk that hits like iron"; his was a spring-steel movement that arrived like a rose and braced like iron. He was a pilot in the Pacific in the Second World War. Afterward he stayed on with Claire Chennault, setting up the Flying Tigers in western China. He was inclined toward Chinese culture, respectful of it, but this did not show in our home beyond a dozen or so books, a few paintings in his office, and two guardian dogs at the entrance to the farm. In later years, when I went to China and when I began printing the work of Lao-tzu and Li Po, I began to understand, in a painful way, that I had never really known him.

And, of course, my sorrow was, too, that he had never insisted that I should. My brothers, who died in the same accident with him, were younger, more disposed toward his ways, not as ambitious as I. He shared with them what I had been too proud to ask for.

———

What drew me to reflect on the orchards where I now live was the stupendous play of light in them, which I began to notice after a while. In winter the trunks and limbs are often wet with rain and their color blends with the dark earth; but blue or pewter skies overhead remain visible through wild, ramulose branches. Sometimes, after a snow, the light in the orchards at dusk is amethyst. In spring a gauze of buds and catkins, a toile of pale greens, closes off the sky. By summer the dark ground is laid with shadow, haunted by odd shafts of light. With fall an elision of browns, the branches now hobbled with nuts, gives way to yellowing leaves. And light again fills the understory.

The colors are not the colors of flowers but of stones. The filtered light underneath the limbs, spilling onto a surface of earth as immaculate as a swept floor, beneath the greens, the winter tracery of blacks, under a long expanse of gray or milk or Tyrian sky, gave me, finally, an inkling of what I had seen but never marked at home.

———

I do not know where this unhurried reconciliation will lead. I recognize the error I made in trying to separate myself from my stepfather, but I am not in anguish over what I did. I do not live with remorse. I feel the error only with a little tenderness now, in these months when I find myself staring at these orchards I imagine are identical to the orchards that held my stepfather—and this is the word. They held the work of his hands, his desire and aspiration, just above the surface of the earth, in the light embayed in their branches. It was an elevation of his effort, which followed on his courtesies toward them.

An image as yet unresolved for me—it uncoils slowly, as if no longer afraid—is how easily as boys we ran away from adults who chased us into orchards. They were too tall to follow us through that understory. If we stole rides bareback on a neighbor's horses and then tried to run away across plowed fields, our short legs would founder in the furrows, and we were caught.

Beneath the first branching, in that grotto of light, was our sanctuary.

———

When my stepfather died he had been preparing to spray the filbert orchard. He would not, I think, have treated the trees in this manner on his own; but a type of nut-boring larvae had become epidemic in southern California that year and my brother argued convincingly for the treatment. Together they made a gross mistake in mixing the chemicals. They wore no protective masks or clothing. In a single day they poisoned themselves fatally. My younger brother and a half brother died in convulsions in the hospital. My stepfather returned home and died three days later, contorted in his bed like a root mass.

My mother sued the manufacturer of the chemical and the supplier, but legal maneuvers prolonged the case and in the end my mother settled, degraded by the legal process and unwilling to sacrifice more years of her life to it. The money she received was sufficient to support her for the remainder of her life and to keep the farm intact and working.

We buried my brothers in a cemetery alongside my mother's parents, who had come to California in 1923. My stepfather had not expressed his wishes about burial, and I left my mother to do as she wished, which was to work it through carefully in her mind until she felt she understood him in that moment. She buried him, wrapped in bright blue linen, a row into the filbert orchard, at a spot where he habitually entered the plot of trees. By his grave she put a stone upended with these lines of Jeffers:

It is not good to forget over what gulfs the spirit
Of the beauty of humanity, the petal of a lost flower
    blown seaward by the night-wind, floats to its quietness.

I have asked permission of the owners of several orchards along the river to allow me to walk down the rows of these plots, which I do but rarely and harmlessly. I recall, as if recovering clothing from a backwater after a flood, how my stepfather walked in our orchards, how he pruned, raked, and mulched, how his hands ran the contours of his face as he harvested, the steadiness of his passion.

I have these memories now. I know when I set type, space line to follow line, that he sleeps in my hands.

BARRY LOPEZ is the author of *Arctic Dreams,* for which he received the National Book Award, and several works of fiction, including *Winter Count* and most recently *Crow and Weasel,* an illustrated fable. He lives in Oregon with his wife Sandra, a book artist.

MEMPHIS

Things went along just fine, too fine, the first couple months I knew Suzy. Then here comes Thanksgiving. She was going home to Memphis. What's Luke going to do? Come on to Memphis.

As soon as I said I'd come down, things changed with us. I got a running lecture on how to dress, act, and talk down home. Daddy was some big investment banker, and when you head home, boy, you better have your business straight. For two weeks before Thanksgiving, everything I did was wrong.

OK—this, that, and the other. Don't chew gum. Don't wear sneakers. I told her, I said I wear about a hundred dollars worth of clothes every day, excluding shoes, which she knows. On the other hand, I don't stick out my little finger when I drink a Coca-Cola, either. Oh Luke, you're pigheaded. Well, I'm just saying. We had about two weeks of that.

Suzy had bright blue eyes that were always saying "prove it." She could take care of herself. But when it came to Daddy, she got like one of these people in a religious cult. They seem as normal as potato chips until somebody mentions the guru's name and they start talking about how Swami Ding-Dong changed their life and their eyes glaze over and you can't reach them. She said he was kind of a run-around guy, lots of affairs outside the marriage. But he was supposed to be so tall and handsome that Mama put up with it. I figured maybe he fished or hunted or something. Maybe we could hop in the car and hunt up some bunnies, bring along some beers.

I'm the first one to say I don't always do too great with the parents, but I was going to make Suzy's folks like me if it was the last thing I did. I tried my best those couple of weeks before going down there. I wanted to put her mind at ease. I wore a shirt around the house, didn't eat in bed, but she was just apprehensive. I'd open a beer, and she'd be looking at me, so I'd say something like, "Want to split this with me?" and she'd say something like, "I hope you're not gonna get drunk on Thanksgiving." I said, "How do you figure I run a business with twelve people under me if I don't know how to handle myself." She said, "I don't know."

I've got a good general manager, Bobby, who I can leave things with for a while at a time, so taking some extra days was no problem. The warehouse is in an area they call Death Valley. Basically it's the kind of area where you don't fall asleep with your mouth open unless you want to wake up with no teeth. But Bobby's famous for taking shit from nobody. I had some business in Cincinnati the week before Thanksgiving, and I'm from Cleveland originally, so I figured I'd drive out and spend a few days seeing everybody and then drive down to see Suzy; it's a straight shot from Cincinnati down to Memphis.

I had a great time in Cleveland. Everybody was there—Leaky Lee, Onzie, Brooks Jenkins, Meg Baker. Then I headed down to Cincinnati and the whole bunch of them came down and stayed in my hotel room, acting like a bunch of animals, as my mother used to say, and I ended up pulling into Memphis on three hours' sleep.

I got to the house sometime around three in the afternoon. They live in a brick mansion in a suburb, about an acre and a half of land around it, lots of trees. Pull it together, Luke. Suzy came outside when I drove up, and as soon as she saw me she started giving me this "How could you do this" look. She's got blue eyes that I swear turn bottle-green when she gets mad. All she said—she didn't even kiss me—was "Mama's right inside, waitin' to meet you."

I made my way up to the front door and her mama was there, holding a drink in her left hand. She was younger than I expected, with frosted blond hair. She said, "Hello, Mr. Jackson," with a nice smile and held open the door for me. It was a real big foyer, with a living room off to the left and a stairway with a polished wood railing curving around upstairs.

"I'm sorry Mr. Edwards isn't here right now to greet you. He had to go into town for a few hours." She had a Southern accent like a well-trimmed hedge. "Douglas is around somewhere, but you'll run into him soon enough, I'm sure." Smile. "Well, you probably want to freshen up. Suzy'll show you your room upstairs. Then come down and have a cocktail."

Suzy and I headed upstairs. All the way up, she was hissing at me, talking under her breath: "Couldn't you have gotten cleaned up at least? You smell like a *men's room*."

"What did you want me to do? Take a shower in a water fountain someplace," I hissed back.

"Well, why'd you have to go and get drunk for?"

"A bunch of friends came down from Cleveland. I couldn't tell them to turn around and drive back."

"I suppose they sat on your chest and poured Jack Daniel's down your throat, too."

We got to the room. I set my duffel on the floor, hefted my suitcase up onto the bed, unlatched it, and opened it out. "I'll be fine soon as I get a shower," I said.

She just stood there with her hands on her hips. I took

off my jacket, folded it, and laid it on the bed. She just stood there.

"Hey," I said. "Come on. Aren't you even going to ask me how the trip was or anything?"

She said, "Maybe I'll think about it once you get yourself cleaned up. You better be cleaned up before Daddy gets home."

"Don't worry," I said, turning around to set my wallet and things on the bureau. I put them next to a china music box shaped like a dancing couple; they were dressed in old-fashioned pink and green costumes, like George Washington and his wife. "This is nice," I said, trying to change the subject.

"Daddy gave me that for my twelfth birthday," she said, smiling a little. Then suddenly she got a horrified look on her face.

"What's the matter," I said.

"What did you have to bring that thing for? Jesus God Almighty." She took a step back.

I had forgotten about the gun completely. I carry it all the time when I'm on the road. It's a habit I have from the warehouse. "Forgot I even had it."

"Well, get rid of it. I thought you just kept it at the office."

"Hey—I'm carrying about $10 thousand worth of materials out there in the trunk. I told you about that."

"Well, leave it outside."

"It's illegal to leave it in a car unattended."

"Not in Tennessee it ain't." I had to laugh; she was probably just faking. Had to give her credit for that. Actually, I wasn't sure myself what Tennessee law was.

"It sure as hell is," I said, bluffing. "You go check on that one more time."

"Ah'm not stayin' in this house, and my mama and daddy ain't either, till you git rid of that thang." She was regressing back to her accent, which she did when she got excited.

I just wanted a little peace. So I said, "OK, look. Watch carefully." I pulled the gun out of the waistband of my pants, checked the chamber to make sure a round wasn't up there, then I slid the clip out.

"OK?" I said. "You can hang onto this if you want to." I held the clip out in the palm of my hand.

"I don't even want to touch it," she said, hunching up her shoulders around her ears as if I were sticking a tarantula in her face.

"Fine," I said. "Watch." I emptied all seven rounds out of the clip and put them in my jacket pocket. Then I stuck the clip into one part of my suitcase and the body into my duffel bag. "Happy now?"

"No." She turned and walked out.

OK. Somebody had put a stack of towels on one of the satin chairs in my room, and there was a bathroom right off the room, so I just went on ahead to get myself together. I figured once she saw me looking fresh she'd give it up. A nap was too much to ask for. If I started feeling out of it I had some crystal meth that Onzie had given me.

I got all cleaned up and dressed, hung my jacket in the closet, and headed downstairs.

Mama had a tray of hors d'oeuvres laid out on the coffee table in the living room. A thick dark green carpet covered the floor; it was like walking on a golf green. There was a fire going, crystal chandelier, all beautiful upholstered furniture. Over the fireplace they had one of those polished convex mirrors with a gold eagle on top. Mrs. Edwards greeted me with a smile. Suzy stood up, too. She had calmed down a little.

"What can I make for you, Mr. Jackson?" Mama asked.

"Please call me Luke, ma'am. I'll just have whatever's handy," I said.

"Now, don't be that way," she said. "Anything you'd like just say it."

"Well, how about a gin and tonic," I said.

"That's Mr. Edwards's drink," Mama said, smiling.

"I'll make it, Mama," Suzy said, and headed out back through a doorway.

A few paintings—portraits and hunt scenes—hung in different spots. One was a big portrait in oil of Mama.

"That was me," she said, "when I came out. I was a little debutante, only seventeen. Over there is Suzy's grandfather, Mr. Edwards's father. This small one over here is of Suzy and Rebecca. That was painted when Suzy was ten and Rebecca eight."

Suzy brought me the gin and tonic, and right then her ten-year-old brother walked into the room, wearing gray flannels, a pressed white shirt, and a blue blazer, accompanied by a black nanny.

"And this is Douglas," Mrs. Edwards said.

"Hi, Douglas," I said. The nanny left the room. He was a good-looking kid. Didn't smile.

Suzy said, "Doug, this is Luke."

He walked over to me, looking me in the eye, until he was about a foot away from me. Then he socked me as hard as he could in the thigh. It hurt like hell, and I was so surprised that I yelled out "Ow!" before I checked myself.

"Douglas!" his mother said. "What kind of a way is that to behave?" Suzy had turned red as a radish. "Luke, I am sorry."

"Oh," I said, "it's no problem. Want to try that again?" I stuck out my hand for him to shake. He took it, pumped up and down twice, like he was pumping for water, then just stood there. Not a word, through the whole thing. "All *right*," I said. The thigh hurt like a bastard. "You pitch for the baseball team or anything?" I asked him. "You've got a heck of a windup."

He shook his head no. OK, I thought. That's all you get.

I started to turn to Suzy and her mom, and he said, "I've got lizards."

Finally something to grab onto. "Oh yeah?" I said. "Catch 'em yourself?"

"Yeah," he said. "Wanna see 'em?"

"Don't bring out those things," Suzy said.

Mrs. Edwards added, "Maybe Luke will look at them after dinner."

I remembered what Suzy had told me, when she said she had a ten-year-old brother: "He's crazy."

"All ten-year-olds are crazy," I had said.

"Maybe he's just kind of wild, then. I don't think Daddy and Mama expected him. There's seventeen years between him and Becky. Daddy hasn't got the heart to crack the whip on him like he should."

Just then Mr. Edwards swept into the room from the kitchen, wearing a gray topcoat. He was skinny and tall, clean shaven, with gray hair waved and pomaded. Mama and Suzy looked like the President of the United States had just walked in.

"Frances," Mrs. Edwards said.

"Hello, darling," he said. He leaned down and kissed her on the mouth and held it for a couple of seconds. Suzy was looking at me expectantly, and I gave her a wink.

When he was finished with Mama, he turned to Suzy and said, "Hello, sweet." She turned her cheek to him and he kissed it.

"Daddy, this is Luke."

"Yes. Welcome, sir. It's a pleasure to meet you. Have these girls been taking good care of you?"

"Just fine, sir," I said, shaking his hand. "Thank you." His face was thin, with high cheekbones, and his hands were manicured. He had Suzy's flashing blue eyes, and skin you could almost see through. He was no outdoorsman. Definitely a dinner-party playboy.

"Well," he said, taking off his topcoat, which Suzy took

from him and went to hang up, "do you need a refresher?"
I had gone through my whole drink.

"Yes, thanks," I said.

"Gin and tonic?"

I nodded, and he said, "Splendid. That's my drink,
too." We walked together toward the bar, which was behind the couch and under the portrait of Suzy and her
sister.

He handed me a fresh drink. It was almost straight gin.
He took a long pull on his, with his eyes closed. "Have
you ever had this?" He pulled up a bottle of gin of a brand
I'd never heard of, from India.

We sat down on the couch, which I sank into like it was
a marshmallow. I told him a little about the trucking business, which he seemed to be interested in hearing about.
He had a funny way of listening; it was like he was reading
my lips. Doug had disappeared; so had Suzy and Mrs. Edwards. I figured they were in the kitchen.

"You know, I've always loved to travel," he said. "I feel
at times as if I've had quite a sedentary life, although goodness knows we've gotten around. We visited Burma last
year. Strictly vacation. I was there for a week before Anna
joined me. Quite good sport," he said, flashing his blue
eyes at me.

"Were you hunting or fishing at all?"

"My Lord, no. I did some fishing as a boy, but I don't
think I'd know one end of the rod from the other today.
The fishing rod, that is. As far as hunting, I never have
tried it. I have been reading the biography of Hemingway
by this man Berger. Have you read it?"

"No, sir," I said.

"Call me Cap, please. No, I am quite fascinated by that
kind of a life—shooting and drinking and going to Africa
and all that. I'm more of a tennis player, I suppose you'd
say. Do you play tennis?"

"I've done it a few times," I said. "I'm not too great at it."

"How long will you be staying with us? Perhaps we'll play some tomorrow."

"I guess through the weekend, if that's OK."

"Stay the month, son. Anna," he called out. "Anna."

Mrs. Edwards came in from the kitchen. "Yes, darling."

"Do we have that time booked at the Reserve tomorrow? Mr. Jackson and I are going to play some tennis."

"I think we have the three o'clock time, as usual. What a nice idea. Are you a tennis player, Luke?"

"As I just told Mr. Edwards, I haven't really played much. I know how, though."

"Well, I'm sure you'll have a good time. I think that's lovely. I'll call the Reserve and double-check the time, Frances. Dinner will be served in about two minutes; Mayanne is just putting the finishing touches on the salad."

"Wonderful," Dad said, as she left the room. "I'm a very lucky man," he said, with a satisfied smile. He stood up. "Have a refresher?"

"No, thanks, sir. I'm doing fine," I said. I was pretty much whacked.

"And please call me Cap," he said, pouring himself another stiff one. "You make me feel antediluvian."

Before we went in to dinner I figured I'd go upstairs and throw some water on my face again, and I excused myself. So far, so good, I thought. Daddy seemed to like me. That was what was important. Suzy had gotten real daughterly, polite, didn't say hardly anything. I kept looking at her like, "How am I doing?" but it was Daddy's show all the way. That was fine, though. The alcohol factor was a little hard to believe.

When I got to my room, Douglas was standing outside the door, staring up at me.

"Hey, Douglas," I said. "How ya doin'?"

"I'm not Douglas," he said. This kid, I thought, is full of surprises.

"Sorry about that. Who are you?"

"I'm Dick Tracy."

"OK, Dick," I said. "I'm going to wash my hands before dinner. How about you?"

"No," he said, taking a step backward.

"OK," I said. I walked into my room and left the door open, and he followed me in and sat on the bed. I looked at him in the mirror as I was washing my hands; he was just sitting there watching me like I was the first halfway exciting thing that had happened in months. "I bet it gets pretty lonely around here sometimes, huh?" I said. Then I added, "Dick?"

He nodded his head up and down exaggeratedly. "Can we go on an adventure?" he said.

Adventure, I thought. "Sure," I said. "What kind of adventure?"

"Let's go in my parents' room and search for evidence."

"Hmmmm," I said. I dried my hands and walked back into the room. He was looking around at my stuff. I felt sorry for him. He was stuck here with his mom, his nanny, and his father, who was definitely a mixed message as a role model. They probably never paid any attention to him. He needed somebody to take him around and show him how to do guy stuff.

"I tell you what," I said, "why don't we go eat, and maybe later on we can go outside and I'll show you some wrestling moves." We could do them on the lawn. If Suzy didn't like it, tough.

"No," he said, with a whine in his voice. "I want to have an adventure."

"OK," I said. He looked like he was getting cranked up to throw a shit fit. "We've got to go eat first, though. After dinner we'll go off someplace and have an adventure. OK?" He nodded kind of absently. "Come on, Dick," I said. "Go on get ready for dinner."

We walked out of the room and I closed the door. He ran down the hall and I walked downstairs. Dougy was a tough case, no question about that. Daddy and Suzy were still talking in the living room. As soon as I got there, Mrs. Edwards came out and called us to the table. We walked through the foyer, into the big dining room, where a table had been set under a chandelier. The silverware was sparkling. Daddy was going to sit at the head of the table nearest the kitchen, Suzy on the left nearest the foyer, and Mrs. Edwards on the right. I was seated at the opposite end, with my back to a large bay window. It was dark out. There was one place open, on Suzy's side, next to Daddy.

"Olive," Mrs. Edwards said. In a moment the nanny appeared. "Can you tell Douglas to come to the table, please."

With that, Douglas ran around the corner and into the room.

"Douglas, don't run in the house," Mrs. Edwards said.

"Where'd you get off to?" Olive said.

"Look what I found," Douglas said. His hair had gotten messed up and he was minus the blazer. He opened both hands and revealed, with everybody craning to look, two hands full of bullets. Everything stopped.

After a second or two, Mrs. Edwards said, "Where in God's name did you get those things?" She looked at Olive and said, "Has Wendell been by here again?"

"No, ma'am," Olive said. "I haven't even talked wit' him." Then, to Douglas, she said, "Where'd you get those at?" Mr. Edwards was frowning slightly, staring at the bullets.

"I found them in a coat hangin' in one of the closets," he said.

"What coat?" Mrs. Edwards said. "No one in this house owns a gun. I want to know where you got those."

This wasn't a good situation. I had to say something. Make it good, Luke. "I better explain," I said.

I told them about how I have to carry the gun for work, and about Death Valley. Just so they didn't think I was blowing things out of proportion, I told them about the time three guys broke in the back windows and Bobby got one of them spread-eagled face down on the ground, with his Magnum pointed at the back of his head, and made the guy's friends stack up a whole afternoon's worth of boxes. I almost told them the pit-bull story, but I figured they might not be ready for that one. Then I said I had taken the gun apart upstairs and put the bullets in the jacket pocket. I said the bullets had probably just fallen out and Dougy must have just found them on the floor.

"I found 'em right in your pocket," Dougy said, suspiciously, as if I were trying to get away with something. "They didn't fall out."

They sat there staring at me for a minute or two, except for Suzy, who wouldn't look at me. I figured maybe they might be a little embarrassed that their son had gone through my stuff, but that didn't seem to occur to them.

"Mr. Jackson, I have a request to make," Mr. Edwards said. "I'd very much appreciate it if you would keep the weapon outside in the trunk of your car. I'll take full responsibility in the unlikely event that something happens and the gun is discovered there while you are here."

"I'd be glad to do that. I brought it in without really thinking." I started to get up.

"No, no . . . please wait until after dinner. Yes, sit down. Thank you."

We just sat there and ate. I tried to catch Dougy's eye, but he had gotten quiet and stayed busy eating. Nobody talked. Every once in a while, Daddy's eyes would flick up from the tablecloth to my face and focus. But most of the time he just sat there with his finger across his lip. Suzy was treating me like I was a complete stranger.

I tried to think if there was any way to make things better. After a while I gave up on that and thought about mixed nuts for some reason. I started thinking about what the best nuts were, in order. You have cashews, peanuts, almonds, pecans, Brazil nuts, and the little round ones. Filberts. Then I had this thought that they were like the properties in Monopoly. Like peanuts were the slums, almonds were the light blue ones, filberts were the railroads, then cashews were the red ones, pecans were Marvin Gardens, and Brazil nuts were Boardwalk and Park Place. After that, I tried to remember the names of everybody in the Addams Family.

After dinner we went into the living room for coffee. Everyone was still acting uncomfortable. Suzy was avoiding looking at me, like I had herpes of the eyeballs. Finally I figured things weren't going to get any better the way they were headed, so I said, "Look, I'll be glad to do whatever I can to get things back on track so we don't have to sit here staring at the rug all night. Like I said, I carry it in my job. I wish I didn't have to, but that's where I am."

Everybody just looked at me kind of surprised for a minute. Suzy licked her lips and looked through me. Mrs. Edwards smoothed her dress and looked at Daddy-o and said, "I think we're not too used to this sort of thing. Nobody's blaming anything on you, Luke; I think we were just a bit taken aback."

"Maybe we ought to play a game or something. We could loosen up," I said. After a second or two, Mrs. Edwards said, "Well . . . that might be a good idea. Suzy, do you still have your Parcheesi board upstairs that you and Rebecca used to play on all the time with Papa?"

"Whatever happened to conversation, I'd like to know," Daddy said. Everybody looked at him now. He had really been putting away the wine at dinner, and now I realized he was looped. "We're not really game players, I suppose, Mr. Jackson."

"Does that mean we're not playing tennis tomorrow?" I said.

"Tennis is a sport, not a game."

"Hey, I tell you what," I said, "I hear you're kind of a sport yourself."

Nobody said anything. Daddy's face turned the color of boiled shrimp. Come on, I thought, say something smartass. This was more fun than staring at the rug. Old Olive was standing by the door of the living room, and I lifted my cup to her. She didn't move a muscle in her face, just turned and walked away.

Right about then I began to think about where I would spend the night. There had to be millions of small hotels in Memphis, and I figured I'd just take off, probably. This whole thing had started on the wrong foot, and it was going to stay there. It was just bad luck, and probably wasn't supposed to work out. I said, "Excuse me for a minute," and got up like I was going to the john.

Upstairs I got my stuff out of the bathroom and threw it in the duffel. It had started raining outside; I wouldn't have to drive too far, at least. I put a few other things back in the suitcase, including a sweater she had given me for my birthday. I checked the dresser drawers, then I pulled my jacket out of the closet and looked around some more to make sure I wasn't leaving anything. I checked the nightstand one last time. Then I just stood there for a minute or two. I felt like I could take off my tie for the first time since the whole Thanksgiving business came up. I had crossed the line and there was nothing left to worry about. I wasn't particularly happy about it. I wondered how anybody ever worked anything out. Learning how to be with someone was like leaving a trail of crumbs leading into the woods; the storm comes and blows the trail away, and next time you have to make the same exact mistakes. I saw myself in a small, chilly hotel room off a fluorescent-lit corridor, trying to sleep and listening to the retching of the ice machine down the hall.

Right then Suzy walked into the room, without knocking, which is standard. I started zipping up the zippers on my bag.

"I'm packing as fast as I can," I said.

She stood there watching me; I could feel her eyes on the side of my head. The room had gotten hotter.

"You," she said, in a hoarse voice, more like a croak, "aren't going anywhere."

I looked up at her; her eyes were puffy, like she'd been crying. "What are you talking about?" I said. "Your mama and daddy think I'm some kind of serial killer."

Her lips were pressed tight together, and she didn't look at me. Instead she reached over to the bureau, picked up the china music box I had noticed earlier and, grimacing, threw it; it grazed the nightstand, then it hit the floor, breaking, behind the bed. "They'll get over it," she said, in a raw voice, looking at me now as if she thought I was playing dumb and forcing her to tell me something I already knew. "It ain't the end of the world." 🍃

TOM PIAZZA's short stories have appeared in *The Quarterly* and *Story,* and his journalism and criticism in *The New York Times Magazine* and *Book Review, The New Republic, Playboy, The Village Voice,* and elsewhere. He is the author of *The Pantheon Guide to Jazz.* Mr. Piazza is currently a Maytag Fellow at the Iowa Writers' Workshop.

JOHN ROLFE GARDINER

THE MAGELLAN HOUSE

*J*n the early years
the Mouras went to Santo Antônio do Porto only in June
when their vacation cottage could be kept a whole month
for the price of a banker's dinner in Lisbon. It was a full
morning's journey there in the aging Renault with luggage
strapped to the top and fishing rods through the windows.

The annual respite from the work year must have gone
back beyond Polegar's clear memory to a time when he
thought "damn it" meant get in the car and shut up, and
his sister Christina's moments of affection were still cherished. Leaving the hot dust of the south for their perfect
bay on the Atlantic Coast, he pitied the cork and eucalyptus trees rooted in place as the car rolled on, past castles
and goatherds.

By the time he was nine and Christina sixteen, the vacation seemed more desirable than ever. The lower street
and public square of the village would be covered with
carnival rides, stalls, and attendant gypsies, and cabanas
strung along the beach like endless rows of playhouses.
But the trip that year was a trail of ill temper, with stops
for threatened beatings. All, he believed, caused by his sister's nasty faces, her rearrangement of luggage in the back

78   *American Short Fiction, Volume 1, Number 4, Winter 1991*
© *1991 John Rolfe Gardiner*

seat to her advantage, and little cruelties too subtle for the court of family justice.

Like other children, he called his parents Mãe and Pai; devotion and obedience built into the very sounds. So why should his name come from *pulga,* the flea, to *polegar,* the thumb and nail that squash it. Diminutive, pesty, it would never have been allowed by the censors in the Civil Registry where he was officially José Ricardo Moura. Too late. His schoolmates had hold of Polegar and would not let go.

What chance against Christina María Santa Veronica de Jésus, favored with a whole church calendar of suffering and adoration. Only a child like himself, he'd thought, but already in the long body of a woman who had arrived at knowledge she could not share. She called him Pulga for short, let her hair down in school against their mother's order, and lied in church.

"Father, I have nothing to confess, unless it is my pride in being able to say so." Polegar had sat in a pew next to her confessional thrilled by the chance she took with her soul. As if she'd not taken coins that week from Mãe's offering box. He hadn't reported her and might be trifling with his own salvation on her account. She was a caution to them all. Mãe had said so.

"Pai," Christina probed on the road, "the men you despise so much, don't they have names?"

"Christina!" Mãe's shrill warning from the front seat bought ten kilometers of silence. Pai spat out the window as they passed the army barracks, and then they were in the town called Baths of the Queen.

Here soldiers on short leave walked through the park with loaded pistols on the hip, the public security forces went by twos, and any man in an ill-fitting jacket was concealing a shoulder holster. And here they stopped each year to use the public toilets, and for Pai to go around the corner for the ritual gift—the cherry liqueur his wife took as her digestive after seafood. A sweet red syrup against the black ink of squid.

"Shall I open it now, Anna?"

"Not in front of the children, Paulo!"

She slapped Pai's naughty hand, and Christina groaned. As if she and Polegar didn't know the local brand of *ginja* came already decanted in a smooth ceramic phallus, upright, circumcised, and looking for all the world like anatomical Easter chocolate. In Santo Antônio it would be put on a high shelf, out of sight.

A half-hour later they were in the crystalline microclimate of the village they loved. For Polegar, who had seen an aerial photo, Santo Antônio was a protractor like the one carried in his school kit since first grade, still unused. Its curve was a two-mile semicircle of white sand, and its straight edge, the line of cliffs over the Atlantic with a narrow cut in their center allowing the ocean in to touch the beach.

In the protected bay, so perfectly shaped and commodious it was called the Marquesa's Bidet, the surf was only a gentle lapping. Once a resort to royalty, Pai explained, now to the privileged, who looked down from their manor houses on the hillside over the quay, their holidays charmed by the fishermen and small merchants far below.

The Mouras' cottage was theirs by informal covenant, too old now to be broken. It had been servants' quarters to the grand old majolica-tiled house above it. Senhor Carvalho opened the small cottage only in June, suffering them into the playground of the wealthy, as it were, through a back door. His wife would appear in the cottage two or three times during the month to ask what was needed. Actually, according to Polegar's mother, to check on breakage.

The two Carvalho boys were not to be trusted at all, she

said. Irreligious, private-school sneaks, each with his own little sailboat, one blue, one red. Polegar watched them dart back and forth on the bay as if it were the water of their own yacht club, narrowly avoiding the fishing boats. The older one, Pedro, Mãe accused of staring impertinently, and Maximino, she maintained, would not look her in the face. Polegar saw the contradiction; Christina dared to speak it: "What are they supposed to do with their eyes?"

That June, the boys' younger sister Inés was the first Carvalho to greet them. Like Christina, sixteen. An appropriate friend, Mãe said, for her daughter, and the only Carvalho child she could really trust. Inés had once taken Christina into the big house, off limits to the rest of them. It has four baths, Christina had reported, and more. Inés had her own room with a little crystal chandelier and doors that opened onto a private balcony overlooking the bay. The dining-room table reflected silverware from the sideboard, and the room's white wood trim shone with the depth of enamel.

Passing on the sidewalk, his mother would touch one of the lovely tiles that covered the mansion from ground to eave, and moan as if pained afresh by their beauty. The way the blue design bled into white, each square a separate masterpiece. If Polegar slid his hand over them it was just to wipe a little snot from his fingers.

The Magellan house, they called it, though how the Carvalho portraits on the paneled walls might connect the family with the great navigator had not been explained. Didn't every town on the Portuguese coast have a family who claimed to live in the Magellan house?

Even so, the Carvalho pretension was a comfort to the Mouras. It pleased them in their tight though adequate space to have something to snicker at. Polegar's father had tried to describe how thin a trace of Magellan blood anyone could claim after the meandering of twenty-five generations.

Polegar knew long before his mother that Inés was not to be trusted, that her church-scout uniform with its brown scarf and green jumper was a disguise for other activity. She bought magazines that had to be carried from the newsstand in brown wrapping, and went off to swim at forbidden beaches up the coast where Pai said the undertow could pull you all the way to America. Polegar could imagine Inés washing up on the hook Massachusetts stuck into the ocean, the place where his cousins lived.

Christina had resisted Mãe's push toward the daughter of the fancy house. Lucky for Christina. If she kept her distance from the rich girl, they could all return from vacation alive. But this year he saw immediately it was going to be different. When Inés entered the cottage her eyes met Christina's with a knowing glance, and his sister asked to be excused from family plans so she might walk the village with her friend.

"What's your father humming?" Inés was alert.

"His revolutionary anthem." Christina's honesty startled them all, and Inés, having discovered a pit, was not afraid to look for snakes. "What are the words?"

"Christina! What rubbish! There are no words, dear," Mãe assured the inquisitive girl.

Polegar remembered asking, "If there aren't any words, how can it be an anthem?" though he'd known there would only be trouble in that direction. With his sister gone he'd have to play on his mother's nerves until he too was released into the village. And though she slapped his face, he was sorry for provoking her. Polegar understood this was the place they came to escape his father's silent rage, where neither He Who nor the pope need be mentioned for a whole month.

He Who, short for he who dictates, was family code for

the prime minister, also called "our economic genius" by Senhor Moura, who worked eleven months of the year as foreman in a ceramic block factory. He had chronic bronchitis, and made half the salary of an ordinary soldier in He Who's army, and a quarter the pay of one of his secret police. His bitterness had been struck into Polegar not with ranting but with a soft and repetitive tapping, as if a stone cutter had been working privately on a message for the ages—This is what happened to me.

Twenty years earlier as a boy of eighteen, Polegar's father had been in the Rossio station in Lisbon, late at night, waiting with two friends for the train home to Torres Vedras. All in high spirits after a picture show. Another boy joined them, and at once they were arrested by He Who's police. A gathering of four after curfew was, on its face, a conspiracy. They were held overnight, questioned, and beaten for their attitudes. After that Polegar's father was on a list to be questioned at any time, hauled in without warrant. "Why would they need a paper from a judge? They arrest judges, too." The spite had to be squeezed through tight lips.

In Santo Antônio the anger could drain away with the tide. Here, Pai went surf fishing with cronies from the market, grilled sardines with the construction workers in the lower town, and built a smile on the dark wine they poured from gallon jugs.

In Santo Antônio his father shed the year's defensive skin. He even brought his shortwave radio out of its box, and allowed Christina to tune in Radio Free Portugal after dark. Christina, who shook her long black hair to rock music via Morocco, refused to translate lyrics for Polegar. Or for her parents.

His sister was the only one of them with enough English to blush at the words. Between the songs were messages in Portuguese, seditious news which Mãe pretended not to hear and which Christina dismissed for impotence. And Polegar saw it was his sister who made the family different. Not only because her wide, round eyes and lithe figure could turn a head.

It was her mind, which darted here and there, stunning her teachers, winning all the prizes in their school. Grabbing the answer to a math problem from the air before the pencils tapping around her touched paper. Spitting history's dates like so many grape seeds. And ready that season to bolt into political insolence. Pai was challenged to keep up.

———

In Santo Antônio they lived behind the shield of their landlord's wide influence. Though they despised the Carvalho fortune built on thousands of acres of grapevines and implicit homage to He Who, they could still relax in the good graces of power. For Christina to take up with Inés, Mãe seemed to believe, would be all to the good. For her daughter's political and Christian soul, an island of safe thought.

"Go ahead, and mind what Inés tells you," as if Inés would know better rules of decorum than Polegar's mother. So like her to be muttering "no better than we are" as she made the extra kettle of potato soup that Christina would be told to carry up to the big house—first gift in the month's little war of pleasantries. While Mãe cooked she'd try to be angry at "the kind of waste going on up there," the quantity of beef and cod thrown into garbage cans.

She probably resented never being asked into the big house. She reproached the ease of wealth but longed for a look at the master bathroom where, according to Christina, the bidet, carved from a single piece of marble, had a frieze of angels below the rim, their eyes raised to the steamy world above. Mãe believed the way into the Magellan house, moated with formality, was over the bridge of Inés's friendship, and this June Christina might at last oblige her.

———

Set free, Polegar followed the trail of the two girls down the steep cobbled walk, past the wide platform of the Super Troll, central attraction of the carnival, the bumper car ride. Each June his sister was "Super Troll" in the family. The name only meant the irresistible beggar she became each night without the fare to ride.

The concessions were closed for the afternoon, and he went to investigate a gathering of older men and women at the beach wall. A fishing boat was being hauled from the water by oxen, but no one paid attention. Ladies had their backs to the sand. He overheard "four Canadian women . . . the police have been called," and then someone reached out, trying to turn his head away from the bay. There, bobbing in the water with breasts uncovered, were the four from Canada, flouting the law of He Who's beaches. And sitting far out on the sand, chins on their knees, taking it all in, were Christina and Inés.

More than enough news to report back to the cottage if it had not been more important to keep his sister in sight. Two police had arrived. Watching through the cold lens of duty, they spoke only to each other, and moved off again. With that, the people's vigil lost virtue; they began to drift away. He hid in wait behind the wall until Christina and Inés began their walk home.

He knew precisely the distance he must keep. Far enough behind not to provoke Christina, and close enough to miss nothing she said, though she was mostly listening to Inés. "Where we go in France they all swim that way."

"The police did nothing."

"Of course not." Inés, bored with the obvious, nevertheless explained why the government did not want tourists bothered, and Polegar followed the two girls up the hill. Christina was being asked up to the big house again; he was shunted off on the cottage path. The news he was bringing home, reduced from shocking to ordinary, went dry, and "nowhere" was the answer to "where have you been?"

————

At dark the carnival machinery began to turn, recorded music boomed up through the stone alleys, and thousands of lights blinked in the undulant motion of the rides they decorated. A time of wild need when deals could be struck with little effort. Pai came across with the coins. In return, Christina pledged deeply, repeating after him: "To keep Polegar with me at all times. To treat him with honor as my own blood."

Her style on the Super Troll was all her own. She rode with a chin-up, how-dare-you face, as if the cars had not been designed for collision. Fingertips on the wheel and elbow resting on the frame, she must have imagined herself parading in a sports car too fine to be scratched. Polegar was used to waiting for the crash.

That night it was Pedro and Max Carvalho from the blind side, with Pedro, the older one, steering. Riding alone, Christina was no match for the momentum of their calculated impact. Her head snapped forward, and she was led off with a bloody lip. Bad fish to Pedro Carvalho.

The year before, hadn't he injured a swimmer, a village girl, with the centerboard of his sailboat? Pedro, one of the handsome boys from Oporto, too rich to be held to account. He seemed puzzled by Christina's accident. Too late with his apology. She was moving away through the crowd.

This time there was valid news to bring home. Something to put the vacation in order, and bring his sister back into the safety of the cottage. Again, he'd misjudged. His mother only moved for reconciliation. "You mustn't judge Inés by her brothers," and his father was equally obtuse. "If I were a young man, wouldn't her car be just the one to aim at?"

Without asking, Christina took the shortwave set to her bedside and tuned in the bad signal. With her swollen lip and rage, she made a splendid martyr, turning the poisonous noise up to the world that abused them. So loud they might hear it through the windows of the Magellan house.

Mãe hurried to Christina's side with the glass of water she always placed on the playing radio.

"Not thirsty."

"Not for you, dear." She reached down to touch the swelling.

"I've told you that doesn't work," Pai called from the other room. "You might as well crawl all the way to Fatima."

Clear enough what was happening. His Pai and sister outdoing each other to prove their courage, while Mãe prayed for their safety and maneuvered for the kind regard of the Carvalho family.

Let the water stay, Polegar pleaded silently, as if a glass of water might keep the wrong people from the door and save the vacation from disaster. From his bed across from Christina, noises off and lights out, he heard the good murmuring and the pouring of the *ginja* that would send his parents giggling off to their own kind of sleep.

The next morning Senhora Carvalho sent her housekeeper down with two blouses: "She thought these would be nice for your Christina. How is her face?" Castoffs of Inés, a little circle of grease on the collar of one, buttonhole torn on the other. From Pai a fist and forearm right up to the elbow for the condescension. The lady didn't see it.

Into the trash with the gifts? No, because the poor woman also brought the summons so long wished for by

his mother: "Senhora says you will come for dinner tomorrow. All of you, yes?"

———

So much to do, Mãe complained. What flowers to take?
Wine? Oh, I wouldn't know what kind! What dress to
wear? What clothes to put on you children?

"Wine? He owns half the grapes in the Douro!" Deter-
mined to make a fool of herself, Pai said. "Dress as we
always dress and take nothing."

Over his mother's protest they showed at the big house
in their usual motley, and were immediately put at ease
by geniality. All so smooth, the Carvalhos gallant to a
fault inside the walls of their intimidating home. Pedro
was scolding himself for a bully, insisting on Christina's
pardon, leading her off to a grassy terrace. Max brought
out cards, and sat down to play with Polegar as if really
pleased to be matching wits with a provincial child, and
Mr. Carvalho put a drink in Pai's hand, inviting opinion
of the new gypsy camp. "Part of the cost of living in
Europe?"

Polegar saw he could whip Max at the game if he chose.
More important to catch everything his father said. The
magnificent house might have gone unremarked in the
sudden Carvalho graciousness, but the Senhora and Inés
had moved quickly to oblige his mother's curiosity. They
led her away, agape at the artful detail in the high plaster
ceilings. And Senhor Carvalho had a little confidence for
his father. "You know, we have a shortwave, too. One
can't stop children from hearing other opinions. Some
things will have to change, don't you think?"

"What I think wouldn't count for much." Polegar
watched Pai drink deeply and extend his glass in friendship. "My wife thinks if you put a glass of water on the
radio, the security can't tell what signal you're listening to."

88   *American Short Fiction*

The two men chuckled.

"Where did she hear that?" Carvalho asked.

"On the Russian station. The one from Czecho-slovakia."

"But why would the Russians put their friends at risk here? Why help our government?"

Cued for a favorite observation, his father couldn't stop himself. "Left, right, they mean nothing. One tyranny will always support another."

Senhor Carvalho was nodding and wondering aloud what good could come of the latest trouble at the local barracks. Pai's face went blank, as if his political stripe were not already clear on his sleeve. And Mãe returned whispering it was true. Angels were circling the bidet.

———

One visit had turned the remote family into confidants. All following the lead of Senhor Carvalho who seemed to have found an attractive mischief in his tenant. A dozen years of distance set aside with a few impetuous words. Now he was coming to the cottage to ask Pai up for the evening beer. "Bring the little boy with you. Maximino likes playing with him." Easy to rout the dull-witted Max at his silly card game, and a bore to let him patronize in false victories.

Senhora Carvalho found new time for his mother, encouraged her to come by in the afternoons to walk on the meadows below the cliffs, and share the pleasures of an amateur botany. Where Mãe had been satisfied with the red glory of poppies waving on the hillside, she was now directed to manifold secrets under that gaudy carpet.

She came home with new veneration for her landlady and fragile petals to press between the pages—of what? No dictionary of flora in the cottage. No bookshelves. Only a magazine rack. And from her husband, a snort if a pale specimen fell into his lap as he leafed through an old number.

———————

Worst for Polegar was the sudden loss of Christina to the team of Inés and Pedro. Perhaps they saw that his sister might be beyond reach of their wealth. They began to take her everywhere with them. Gave her lessons in how to be rich—how to hold a cup of espresso, a cigarette, the tiller of a sailboat.

Inés's cool, oval face was treated with softening lotions, and colors brushed about the eyes from a rainbow of little bottles. This was the ideal held up to Christina. Inés was stepping back from complete self-absorption to a preparation of his sister.

"Look at you, Christina, Pedro thinks you're wonderful, but your skin, so dry!" There were glances behind Christina's back, and whispering.

"Are you ready, Christy?" Inés at the door again, and Pedro, without license, at the wheel of one of his father's cars. "Have you brought the right bathing suit?"

Which meant they were on the way to the wrong beach, where the Canadian women had taken their sport. For the sin of it all, wouldn't the undertow drag someone out to sea?

Polegar couldn't follow, and no one else was home to save Christina. His mother walking with the woman who spoke Latin to weeds, Pai off with boozy fishermen, maybe boasting of his new sway with the landlord whom he'd taught to say "He Who" with a sneer.

They'd been in Santo Antônio little more than a week, and now Polegar was leaving with Pai for the big house each evening after supper. There he'd sit cross-legged on a rug from India opposite Max, who said Polegar would do better if he'd stretch his memory. The men sat above them in deep leather chairs that seemed to absorb harmlessly all attacks on the state. More beer was poured.

"At least," Senhor Carvalho was grateful, "there's the Church for balance."

Pai raised a hand to demur. An institution always falling into the wrong hands, serving the wealth and vanity of the few.

No argument from his host. "All this time, Paulo! Who knew we had so much to share? And the children have finally discovered each other."

———

Later, he could imagine the way Senhor Carvalho would have pulled his chin into a wise point as he gave the orders: Maximino, you'll take on the little one. Let him win on occasion. Pedro, Inés, I trust the two of you can gain the confidence of the proud daughter. (All this and more.) Your mother will distract the Senhora, and I'll handle Senhor Big Talk.

Polegar could not be everywhere at once, couldn't monitor his father's nightly bluster while trailing his sister through the carnival onto the beach, watching her mingle hands and glances with the rich boy turned gallant. Christina bought night freedom from Polegar with Super Troll fare, but small coins could not buy off infinite curiosity. He soon saw how the two ambled off through the shadows to find an empty cabana.

Inés must have known her work was nearly done. He heard her excuse herself: "Pedro needs time alone with you, Christina. I know! Take him into one of the tents. He's much too shy to ask you."

Shy? No trace of self-consciousness before this. In that family only Maximino suffered from self-awareness. His bluff and presumption, all imitation. "Another vapid day in paradise," presented as original malaise, would have been learned an hour earlier from his brother.

It had been Polegar's duty that summer to watch and listen in silence as his father and sister went leap-frogging over one another's nerve. At a discreet distance from the chosen tent he learned that a persuasive lie—"It's all right, Christina. We aren't children."—might be followed by an odd, diminutive moaning, what he would call her squeaking noises when it came time to tell.

Fed up with nightly romance, he had gone again with Pai to the big house where the men had progressed to brandy and the folklore of failed assassinations. "A bazooka would have been easy." His father rising ardently from his chair, whistling his palm through the air in a slow arc. "The Thursday night poker game in the Brazilian Embassy. He Who used to come in the side door. Everyone knew about it."

———

Perhaps Inés understood that time was short. Returning to help her brother and Christina over another hurdle, she had brought her guitar to a tent tryst and plied them with *fados*. All the sad news of incomplete love in her soft, clear voice. Unwanted beach strays gathered to admire.

Another night Senhora Carvalho had pulled the grownups off to a play at the House of Culture in the nearby town. Dumped by the older children, Polegar wandered about the carnival, and came home to a cottage lit by one dim candle. Through the window he saw Christina, Pedro, and Inés sitting down to the kitchen table with the shocking decanter of *ginja* in front of them.

The three were watching one another, motionless, until Inés took her brother's hand, placed it on the clay shaft, and helped him pour for Christina. Nothing was said. And now Inés did the same with Christina's hand, gently guiding it to fill Pedro's cup. Like little gods and goddesses for whom ritual was serious symbol. Polegar reeled off into the sinning night. When he came home again the *ginja* had been put away, the cups were gone and the house empty.

———

At a small hour, still awake on his bed, he listened to his parents prepare sentences of increasing severity for the absent Christina. House arrest, beating, a convent school, which they could not afford.

She came home conceding nothing, though she couldn't deny where she'd been. The smell in her clothes and hair was too heavy to escape Mãe's twitching nostrils. Lying in the rosemary thickets in the high meadows. "You expect us to believe you went alone?"

The household was hardly down to chastened sleep when men came for his father, agents of Mãe's worst daydreams, dressed like fishermen but carrying the feared laminations in fast-flip wallets.

"No rush, Senhor Moura. Our people are not cruel."

He was told to take his wife and children home to Torres Vedras, to wait there. "There'll be time enough to tell us all about the bazooka."

Pacing through the night, Pai promised revenge on the weasel Carvalho. There were some kind of good-byes to be said to the informing landlord, but he and his family had already escaped for their northern residence.

———

Polegar was carsick. What castle? Damn the Moors, damn the Romans, damn the Castilians! Did his mother expect him to think now of distant patriotisms? As if she were interested at that moment in the ancient, shifting tenancies of the walled city they were passing, as Pai drove on, contemptuous, spitting out his window to prove it, toward surrender.

Mãe was frantic, trying to divert herself from the certainty of her husband in a cell. "What did you tell him, Paulo?"

Deflected, she faced Christina in the back seat. His sister, her eyes black with loathing for the family's ignorance, swore her friend Pedro could know nothing of what Senhor Carvalho had done.

"I expect you've got plenty to tell the priest."

"Not a thing," Christina complained, her lip trembling. "There's never anything to tell him."

"What about your squeaking noises in the cabana?" Polegar offered helpfully. "And drinking from the penis."

The car stopped. Pai got out and opened Polegar's door. Taking him by the arm, he marched him off through a eucalyptus glade, far out of sight of the highway.

———

His parents came home to the bitterest month, in which tears and recrimination were not cathartic. The screaming, the slamming shut and throwing open of doors, no relief. Pai returned to work. What else? To run was to put all their lives at risk. Mãe wondered if they'd come for him at the house after dark, or take him from the job. After dark meant no address, no return.

Every day she intruded on Christina's toilet. Christina threw the whole roll of paper at her. Mãe would have been sniffing around for his sister's blood, which was late. Christina's jaw was set tight, as if her summer sport could have been ennobled by her own honest thrall.

Maybe the rest of his sister's body knew more than her stubborn heart. How desperately it must have been working to reject the germ. A spontaneous flow a month later held for Mãe the redemption of God's own blood. Or was she so weepy-smiley because with each passing day her husband was a step further from arrest.

Another scare for He Who at a northern barracks. At the café Pai sat the reborn Christina across from him, poured

94   *American Short Fiction*

her wine, and sang in her face his revolutionary anthem, with words. Mãe beat at his chest, begging him to be still, while Christina raised her glass, saluting audacity. There was a new verse in which tyrants dined on offal, the only remains of their informers.

Christina wouldn't be outdone. She rose in her class-room to give rote on a national fairy tale, the only kind of history allowed. Her instructor waited for the story of a baker woman who pushed a Spanish soldier into her oven, shifting the tide of battle six hundred years ago. Instead, Christina named a revolutionary shot only months earlier. Polegar heard how his sister had been pulled from the room by her ear.

Now he could only admire the timing of Christina's de-fiance, and the lesson of his father's excess: choose that year in the life of a nation when recklessness becomes heroic. The year when carnations are placed in rifle barrels and soldiers are charmed away from one authority into the sway of another.

In the spring, a single general called about face, and forty years were repudiated in a moment. Men with debts of blood and deceit fled the borders. The Moura radio played news of redistribution, of informers going under-ground, or leaving Portugal in fear for their lives. Lifted on the democratic tide, Polegar's family prepared for an-other June in Santo Antônio.

———

This time they entered the cottage like thieves. He was sent through a window to unlock the front door for his family. The Carvalhos were gone, probably following their money to the banks of northern Europe.

For the Mouras it was a time of careless retribution. On the cottage stoop there was a daily grilling of sardines, with old summer friends coming up the hill to drink from a common jug and congratulate the family on their bold entry. Though it was soon clear Pai would not be satisfied with this. Rent-free occupation of the small quarters was too paltry a revenge.

Mãe protested, but the next week Polegar was raised to the balcony of the big house where he forced his way through the glass doors of a bedroom, and felt his way down the grand stairway to let the family in. Valuables and smaller effects were gone, but all the large furniture remained.

Invading every room, they threw shutters and windows open to the sun, tossed themselves on the beds, flopped down on chairs and sofas. Like giddy travelers testing a new hotel for comfort before deciding to spend the night. "Christina, you take the girl's room. Polegar, you'll be at the end of the hall. Anna, what do you think of this bed?"

Mãe, about to live in the house she most coveted, was arguing against it, predicting a summary eviction. Pai swept aside the fears. "The rats have run. The country is ours."

They went back and forth between cottage and mansion for a week or so before daring a full night in the big house. Nothing was said against them. There was only encouragement from other revolutionary spirits in the lower town. And a few days later the occupation was complete.

His sister took it casually. A matter of course that they should be there. For several months she'd been receiving curious notes from Pedro, postmarked Belgium. And they continued to arrive once the Mouras reached Santo Antônio. She would read the family a line or two and keep the rest to herself.

"We hear you've moved into the big house for the month. Whatever my family has done to yours . . ."

From the little she revealed, Polegar supposed that this letter, like earlier ones and those that followed, gave his sister a double pleasure. They seemed to affirm that Pedro

had been *her* fool, and they gave her something of the Carvalhos to tear and burn once flattery had been absorbed.

". . . I will use what influence I have with my father,"
Pedro wrote her. Was this a warning, Polegar wondered,
of trouble if they continued in the house?

Whatever the letters held of teenage mush was her affair.
"Affair, exactly." Mãe found tricky resonance scattered all
through Christina's talk. "Burn before reading," she
warned. Wasn't it proven beyond quibble that teenage
mush was dangerous mush? No end to her suspicion. Why
would the boy keep writing to a silent correspondent?

No more dancing off to the wrong beaches. The two-
piece bathing suit was replaced by one that covered the
shoulders and had a little apron attached that fell to Christina's knees. Under her breath she said if she felt like it
she'd take the whole damn thing off. Despite this, Polegar
believed his sister was grateful for new restrictions that
season, even for chaperoned evenings. That she felt a duty
to heal a shameful sexual scar.

No longer just a summer victory, the estate was a prize
to be held. Though the neighbors would begin to notice
how the gardens were running down, unattended. With
bamboo and brambles crowding up against the terraces.
No one believed Pai's boast. That the place was getting its
just deserts. So that a common man could one day live
here without shame. A common man like himself. He had
found another job with modest pay at a block and tile
company a short distance inland.

For Polegar the house was a troubling surfeit of rooms
where the arrangement of Carvalho furniture dictated the
pattern of the new routine. Mãe found some pleasure in
imitating the privilege that preceded her, though she was
always behind in her new war on dust and mildew as she

went from room to room. Never mind, no bed was moved, not a table shifted.

A novelty to sleep and eat there. Polegar didn't know that the next few years of their lives would be marked by a struggle against decay. The year they let the south-end bathroom go out of use. The summer the damp stain reached half down his bedroom wall. The season they began to find woodworm tailings along the baseboards in Christina's room.

These were uneasy years. Years of waiting for the Carvalhos. And they did come home to Portugal. At first by proxy. All the letters from Pedro, and then the girl's face in a sappy television drama from Lisbon. Christina spotted her and called the family to watch the credits confirm Inés Carvalho was Queen Leonor. Mãe was satisfied there was nothing to admire. "They bought her the part."

Polegar knew the only rent his family paid for the Magellan house was drawn from the balance on a moral debt. The one incurred in the summer of Carvalho treachery. Law and a new class of judges were making long-term squatters difficult to dislodge. Still, his sister was the only one who, as the years passed, felt fully at home here. The one who would be able to tell others about the living-room ceiling.

"A plaster bas-relief with cherubs in the corners holding up a woven garland. The centerpiece is a rose and geranium bouquet." How could she know all that or feel free to tell the world? Polegar never let his eyes linger on the rich surfaces.

Step by step, he could feel the ousted family coming back to them. Senhor Carvalho was seen in the corridor of the regional courthouse in conversation with one of the property lawyers. After that, Mãe assumed every stranger at the door carried eviction papers.

Pedro had written another letter to Christina. "Whatever damage our families have done one another . . ." One of the soft messages that kept coming. His improbable postal suit. Love notes on legal paper?

Neither would the sister fade away. Inés's face insinuating itself over and over again on their television. The glamor press had caught up with her racy biography. Nineteen now, and already two marriages, an alleged pregnancy, intimacy with another actress (photographed).

From moral high-ground they followed her career. Now she was Claudia, antiheroine of a telenovela. The one with the wide mouth painted wider, who had tried to electrocute her man, dropping a lamp in his bathtub. Inés had achieved the gaudy celebrity for which her childhood was rehearsal. A seamless transition to a profession of the way she'd always behaved.

In the periodical literature she was drawn more tragically. Inés, grape heiress manqué. Daughter of the former wine baron with a political side to him. His vineyards lost during voluntary exile after the revolution, the land doled out.

Actually, not so tragic for the Carvalhos, since the whole family was repatriated and doing well again. Even feckless Maximino, who had joined his father in hot coastal development. Senhor Carvalho worked the city in a silk suit, while Max was sent back to Santo Antônio in the baggy flannel of the common man. Here, where his slow mouth, mistaken for innocence, best served the family interest. His job, to promise apartments in beachfront condominiums to those who commit their land to the future.

In Santo Antônio he'd found dozens of ways to avoid Polegar. Simple moves like turning his back, crossing to an opposite sidewalk, hiding his face in a newspaper, ducking into a pastry shop. Or the fictitious loss of a coin, drawing his eyes to the floor.

Pedro was more a mystery. Polegar could only think of him as the shadow that crossed his sister's face when his name was mentioned. Or as the postmark on his letters. And soon enough Pedro's postmark was Portuguese.

Christina had become secretary for the exhibition hall at the House of Culture, and bookkeeper to the ballet instructor there. She was bringing young men home to see the house—dancers and painters who struck poses with dangling cigarettes. They held her hand and looked over the bay from the overgrown terrace. Artists of the fading revolution with the local heroine, the woman who, several years ago, had defied He Who, and claimed the mansion of an informer.

She was making Mãe pay for all that nervous attention to her dress and hygiene, going through her men much too quickly and without real interest. Obvious to Polegar. She encouraged him to come along if they tried to steer her further from the house. These men were not lovers, he was sure, but props brought around to show that an appropriate social need was being met.

"You ought to be getting on with your life," was Mãe's consent to some new passion for Christina. As long as it led to a church. Instead, Christina had settled into a habit of privacy. Setting off to work she showed the hard edge of a woman whose course is set. Wore clothes that straightened her figure, and heels that beat a staccato on the village cobble, warning strangers away.

On market days she went alone to Baths of the Queen, sailing out under false colors as it happened. Got up in the common black of bereavement offset by a white lace collar that might have signified her late commitment to chastity. And carrying a basket that came home filled with chard and kale, salt-cod and turnip greens. As if her only rendezvous in the town had been with merchants, procuring the stuff of a bitter, healthy regimen.

"You could do something with your hair." If Mãe began that way it could turn quickly bitter and confusing.

"There's nothing wrong with you. Hold your head up. Listen to me. And don't play the saint around here."

If Mãe kept on, Pai might give her a sharp tap on the head, and remind them all, "We're here. It's settled," and those people would be coming back over his dead body. Though they'd already invaded the house countless times by mail and television. And a magazine with a photo of the whole Carvalho family gathered in honor of Inés's second wedding, carried up to Christina's room. To laugh at? Stick pins in?

It was still easier for Polegar's father to scoff than relax in the spacious house. "What part Magellan could the people be if the great man himself went to Spain and married a Spanish lady?"

———

A friend of Christina from work had come visiting. A man who'd been the village soccer hero. Letting go of his athletic body gracefully, he spent his free hours at a chess board brooding over the greedy direction the revolution had taken. He appeared with a rose, and recited for Christina from the Czech novel of the season. "Socialism concedes nothing to tyranny."

Maybe, maybe not. But what did this have to do with putting the flower in Christina's hair and kissing her neck? This was a man favored by Polegar's mother, one expected to do the right thing, come to Pai with a confession of his suit and prospects. A local man working on an honest political conscience, on views he must have supposed Christina would admire. She turned him away at the door.

"I don't have time," she said softly, inventing an excuse for this night and one for the next.

"What do you have time for?" Mãe hovering over another lost evening.

Television. They all had time for television. It's the hour

of the telenovela, when they allow Inés into her old living room as electric, colored dots. A smear of red across the mouth, a bronze neck covered with rhinestones, and body wrapped in a tight, blue, silky tube, all moving to a theme of dissatisfaction.

Mãe sits alert, ready to be insulted all over again by Inés's character. And Inés gives her yet another moral victory.

"The part was made for her."

"She made herself for the part."

His mother and sister had even found a way to contest their full agreement.

"The wig is just right for her."

"She makes the wig look right."

The voices took on that edge again, when civility, as a sighing effort, became a provocation.

"Christina, why must everything I say be a target? Am I such a trial to you? Put on something nice, and let your brother take you for a walk."

"Something nice?"

She must have been waiting for that. She ran up to her room and came down moments later to strut in front of them, twirling the two halves of the banished bikini. Mãe dismissed the bathing suit with wistful satisfaction. "She doesn't have the shape for it anymore. She wouldn't wear it."

———

Polegar had imagined Senhor Carvalho living in fear of Pai. Why else had the challenge never come? For how long had they eaten, slept, and moved their bowels here before the first agent of the Carvalhos came to the door?

And what was there to show off to him but mildew in the front hall, and their new ages? His complexion was already clearing. And Christina, grown up, with people beginning to ask Mãe if something were wrong.

Very apologetic, the man had been instructed not to dis-

turb Senhora Moura. "There is a picture of Senhora Carvalho's mother when she was a child. Needed for the cof-
fin." He knew exactly where they should look. "The tall
bureau in the second guest bedroom upstairs. Senhora says
the drawer will stick this time of year."

"I'll have to ask my husband."

Mãe's hand trembled as she pushed the man back from
the doorway. They'd all been warned. Any Carvalho entry, any concession, might have a disastrous consequence.

The next morning Polegar followed Maximino into the
pastry shop, and caught him between the counter and another patron. He'd expected to say, "We're sorry about
your grandmother. Of course your mother is welcome to
the picture." But he was suddenly wary of healing. And
his first words to Max were a false ignorance. "So whatever became of your sister?"

Max, sucking on his teeth, decided, "She's done all
right." And he slid past Polegar with his own arch question. "Which room are *you* using?"

Instead of shouting at his retreat, "Your room, you
prick!" Polegar let the moment evaporate and condense
slowly again into regret.

———

Christina's new wardrobe that spring was not really daring according to the line coming north from Lisbon and
gradually moving up the provincial leg. Mãe, being careful
not to shame her, still coaxed without specificity. "Why
don't you bring one of your nice men around?"

It didn't work that way with Christina. If you walked
along the beach on a Saturday, you would see her out on
the sand in the bikini, alone, reading Pessoa perhaps, or
the fiction of some martyr of the Eastern Bloc. The bathing suit no longer a provocation, even in the family. It was
the common thing now for women from the cities and
tourists to swim topless in Santo Antônio.

Walking out to call her home for lunch, Polegar was shocked to see Pedro Carvalho leaning against the beach wall, turned out in summer whites. And perfectly composed, as if he'd been dropped in from the Riviera to show how this scene could be played with style. No display of silver against a bare chest. Only sunglasses hanging under the one free button of his starched shirt. He stood absolutely still, studying the small area where Christina lay facedown in the sand.

It was apparent she knew she was being observed from the wall. No shrinking into her core of self-contentment. You could see her luxuriating in the attention, taking in warmth at the pores. Wriggling her frontal shape into the loving sand. Her legs bent back at the knee, feet waving a slow semaphore of satisfaction with Pedro's gaze.

Pedro strolled onto the beach and sat beside her. Without looking up, Christina reached out to touch his leg. They hadn't spoken, but now she rolled over to face him, and he leaned to kiss her forehead. Flat on her back, she was poking a finger into the soft, olive skin below her navel, pointing straight down. Reverently, Pedro placed his hand there.

When Polegar turned to leave they were still fixed in that same position of silent worship. He was agape with detail learned from mime alone, the devotion in the soft touch of lips to her brow. Their intimacy as public as the air they breathed. And clear to Polegar, even without the first hint of a swelling, there was going to be a child. That some faint fraction of a Magellan was already waiting in embryo under Pedro's hand.

He hurried up the path, more exhilarated than dismayed. Preparing himself for his parents, projecting into the future: There's a child in my sister's womb waiting a turn to bathe in the Marquesa's Bidet, and make a claim on a birthright home.

He slowed, catching his breath, considering the long deception of Christina's separate peace. But where was the fault in a deception so long anticipated by Mãe's nagging question: Why would the boy keep writing to a silent correspondent? He was like a child again, hurrying home to tell a tale on a slippery sister. This time with news that could not go dry in his mouth.

———

Christina confessed her story in pieces. That afternoon she admitted reacquaintance with Pedro, a season of market-day encounters. By suppertime she told how the two of them had been married a month earlier at the Civil Registry. Not planning to move in together until Pedro found the perfect house. Secrecy had only been meant to save the families from an awkward ceremony.

Perfect house? They knew it wasn't a house she needed. All she needed was for the rest of them to move out of this one. For Pai and Mãe to return to Torres Vedras where they could at last feel at home again.

But why wouldn't a girl so radiantly happy proclaim her pregnancy to the world? She was in no hurry to drive them away. Perhaps Christina didn't announce her condition until she no longer felt comfortable in the bikini. Far enough along that the sequence of marriage and conception, whatever it had been, was blurred by joy and the passage of time.

Mãe made another little show of indignation, though her patience had been winding down to "long enough." Pai had his own way of taming the news. "Haven't I explained it to you? After twenty-five generations we're all related to Magellans."

Within the week they were ready. The departure was dignified. Without tears. He followed his mother and father through the door. Outside, his hand slid along the lovely blue wall in reverence due the home of kin. And Christina waved down to them from her balcony with all the confidence of a clever, fertile queen.   ∙≤ჸ

JOHN ROLFE GARDINER is the author of three novels, a story collection, and a novella *The Incubator Ballroom*. A Creative Writing Fellow of the National Endowment for the Arts, he has been a contributor to *The New Yorker* and many other magazines. In 1989 Mr. Gardiner spent eight months in a Portuguese coastal village similar to the one he describes in "The Magellan House." He lives with his wife Joan and daughter Nicola in Unison, Virginia.

Short Fiction ...

Collected Stories
R. V. Cassill

"Just about every story in this collection is a textbook example of what a piece of short fiction ought to be: immediately engaging, swiftly paced, economical....The premise and development of the stories is almost invariably excellent."
—New York Times Book Review

$29.95 cloth, $14.95 paper

Power Lines and Other Stories
Jane Bradley

"[Bradley's] characters come blazing to life at the most unexpected moments. ... The best stories in **Power Lines** are loaded with terror, wonder, and life—and with promise for Jane Bradley's future."
—New York Times Book Review

$17.95 cloth, $8.95 paper

Back Before the World Turned Nasty
A *Collection of Short Stories*
Pauline Mortensen

"...a certain kind of low-rent survival in the face of breakdown (physical, structural, psychological, regional) is captured precisely here."
—The Kirkus Reviews

$17.95 cloth, $8.95 paper

The Acts of Life
Tales by Tom T. Hall

"...the reader finishes **The Acts of Life** having learned something about the value of love and the story within the story."
—The Tennessean

$12.95 cloth, $7.95 paper

...from Arkansas

The Literary Review turns up in some unique places

AN INTERNATIONAL JOURNAL
OF CONTEMPORARY WRITING

285 Madison Avenue, Madison, NJ 07940

Subscriptions: $18 yearly U.S./$21 elsewhere
Single issues: $5/$6

© LK MCDANIEL 90

University of Texas Press

MAE FRANKING'S "MY CHINESE MARRIAGE"

By Katherine Anne Porter
Edited by Holly Franking
Foreword by Joan Givner

Porter ghostwrote the story of this fascinating and controversial interracial marriage during an era when such relationships were bitterly and publicly discouraged.

ISBN 0-292-75132-X $16.95 cloth

VILLAGE OF THE GHOST BELLS
A Novel
By Edla Van Steen
Translated by David George

Brazilian author and playwright Van Steen's second novel is a fascinating story of a would-be utopian community in São Paulo and its ultimate self-destruction.

ISBN 0-292-73063-2 $12.95 paper

THE REPUBLIC OF DREAMS
A Novel
By Nélida Piñon
Translated by Helen Lane

". . . a masterly tour de force that should establish [Piñon] in the front ranks of Latin American writers." —*PHILADELPHIA INQUIRER*

First published in 1989, this mesmerizing novel marks the debut in English of one of Brazil's most important and critically acclaimed contemporary writers.

ISBN 0-292-77050-2 $17.95 paper

NELSON ALGREN
A Life on the Wild Side
By Bettina Drew

"Drew writes of [Algren] with compassion, understanding, and a keen sense of the all-important social context of his writing. . . . The decline and death of a valuable native literary movement were encapsulated in Algren's life, and Drew has done both man and movement honor." —*PUBLISHERS WEEKLY*

ISBN 0-292-75543-0 $16.95 paper

Available at bookstores or,

 University of Texas Press

Box 7819 Austin, Texas 78713 (800) 252-3206

AMERICAN SHORT FICTION

Laura Furman, *Editor*
University of Texas at Austin

Contents of Next Issue, Number 5, Spring 1992

American Short Fiction, published quarterly in Spring, Summer, Fall, and Winter, is available by subscription. Subscriptions begin with the Spring issue.

Subscription rates: Individuals, $24; Institutions, $36
Outside USA, add $5.50/subscription.
Money order, check or credit card orders accepted.
Prepayment required.

Name _____

Address _____

_____

City _____

State _____ Zip _____

Please charge my subscription to:
_____ VISA _____ MC _____ AM EXPRESS
Account # _____
Exp. date _____
Phone # _____
Signature _____
Total amount enclosed $ _____

Reply to: Journals Department, University of Texas Press,
Box 7819, Austin, Texas 78713